LYCAN

MONSTERVERSE

ALLIE SANTOS

So we all had a thing for the Beast, huh? This one's for all of us who preferred his monstrous form.

CONTENT WARNINGS

Monster-Human Sex, Mention of Human Consumption, Descriptive Murder Scenes, CNC, Forceful Sex Scenes, Knotting, Somnophilia, dubious consent, attempted SA of FMC

Please be advised that the following trigger and content warnings contain spoilers for the story and plot of the novel.

LYCAN is an MF Paranormal Romance. The main characters partake in rough monster sex. The main male monster is not human, and there is reference of him consuming humans in the past. The monster performs multiple acts of *tasting* his human as well as forcing her to taste him, without requesting consent beforehand. The main male monster is primitive and claims the main female character without outright consent various times throughout the book. Toward the end of the book, a side character unsuccessfully attempts to assault the main female character.

LYCAN is set in a mythical world and all contents are pure fiction.

I DUG MY FINGERS INTO THE SOIL, SEEKING OUT THE roots. Potatoes didn't need too much to grow. They were tough little ones. I yanked one up by the stem, dusted off the excess dirt, and tossed it into the woven basket sitting to my left. It thudded on top of the pile.

The sun hung low in the sky, the dark reds and purples signaling the coming darkness. I'd have to return to the house soon or end up spending another night in my shack, just as I'd been taught—just as I'd learned. Under no circumstances were we allowed to be out when it was fully dark out. Even though I'd never seen monsters out here, mountain lions sometimes prowled, and I'd have a significantly lower chance of surviving an attack from them without being able to see. I couldn't be *too* careful. Plus, Jason was extremely protective of me. If he knew I wasn't following the rules and roaming around after dark, I'd never be allowed to leave the house again.

I climbed to my feet with a grunt, stretching my arms up to get the kinks out, then crouched to hug the basket to my chest. I started down the dirt path of the clearing, passing the lines of vegetables and fruits I'd nursed to life.

This patch of the clearing had been the perfect place to relocate my garden to a couple of years ago. On my way out of the green maze, I snagged a cucumber from its stem and popped it into my basket.

Patches of grass littered the walkway I'd burned into the ground. Its clear indentation wove into the break of the forest line. Trees blocked out the rest of the low hanging sun, casting me within the shadows of the pine trees stretching into the sky.

Pam and Jason were likely settling in for the night. I'd left dinner on the stove for them, knowing I'd be heading out until sundown. There was no way they'd be waiting for me, so I took my time, enjoying the cool air fluttering the loose strands of hair around my face.

I tipped my head back, breathing in the fresh air. Something was off . . . The forest was quiet today. Usually around this time of day, the chirps, caws, and flutters of wings filled the woods. I didn't like the extent of the silence, it was odd enough for it to catch my attention. I quickened my pace.

A gust of strong wind loosened more hair from my ponytail until it tickled my jaw and set off the wind chimes hanging from my shack. The glittering pieces hanging on the awning swung side to side with the flurry of wind. The door rocked back and forth. I slowed along the path, frowning. I'd closed it earlier.

Setting my basket down, I hurried up the slight hill, leaves crunching under my leather-bound shoes and thighs burning at the burst of exertion. I climbed up the two wooden steps leading across the five feet of porch to my shack threshold. I caught the door before it thumped against the frame again. Wood chips lay scattered at my feet from the broken knob.

I stepped inside the shadowed room, already sweeping my gaze over the wood table bolted into the wall, looking for the rope I used to secure the door. The small window above the worktable allowed me enough light to see it at the end of the long surface. I beelined toward it, but my toe smashed into something, and I fell to the side and onto my hip. Next to a massive, furry mound.

A scream lodged inside my throat. The mass moved in a rhythmic up and down motion, like it was breathing. I scrambled back so fast, my foot slid across the floor and smacked into it. A pain-filled groan exploded through the room. But the mass didn't lunge at me. I shakily got to my feet and scrambled to grab the matchbox to light my candles, keeping an eye on the *thing* in case it moved. The flame burst to life and cast a glow over my shack. I grabbed the walking stick leaning to the left of the door and held it in front of me.

It was obviously a large animal . . . I squinted. My hands trembled as I lifted the stick and poked it, but there was no reaction from it. I inched near, leaning closer, the smell of pine emanated off the fur. The animal smelled of woods and fresh air. Was it dead? I used the stick to poke it again. Antlers scraped across the ground. I flinched at the sound. Was it an injured buck seeking shelter?

A low unusual glow flared to life throughout the creature's fur—illuminating it. Ears. . . My legs gave out. A large canine maw. This was not a buck or a wolf, this was much, much larger. And scarier.

Ice traveled through my veins, and I couldn't move. My heart pounded so hard that the quick thumps drowned out my breathing. I'd never seen a monster. I struggled to swallow or move.

It was splayed out in a way a wolf could not lay. Its torso stretched out flat, with a wide fur covered chest raising up and down. Barreled arms with joints at the wrist that bent in an inhuman way. The hands were not paw-like, they stretched with four long flanges, thick and long, with deadly-looking claws curving out from the nail bed. A long canine muzzle stretched outward, but it was much larger than a normal wolf's.

Stories about monsters were all I knew about them. Jason and Pam told me how blessed we were to live far from the Rift. How we were lucky to never have encountered them.

My fingertips touched a pool of liquid. I brought them up high to see it. An onyx, almost inky, moisture coated my fingers, the scent smelling heavily of copper. Blood? I trailed my attention over the monster. Upon closer inspection, I noted the fur was matted and damp at the wrists, ankles and neck, the cuts so deep I could see flesh and even bone. I swallowed back a gag.

It was hurt. Was it a male? Bucks had antlers, but there were other species that were both male and female that had antlers.

I'd never seen a monster before, so I was at a complete loss. No, this was an 'it'—a creature I needed to get rid of. My stomach lurched.

As I regained a bit of control, labored breathing reached my ears. I struggled with death. I hated hurting anything living, which was why Jason had to go hunting without me. As much as they'd tried to get me to kill animals, I just couldn't. But would it come after all of us if I did nothing? I struggled to swallow. It would kill us all with a single swipe of its claws. We'd be no match for it.

I stumbled to the side table and plucked the shovel off the counter. Returning to the animal, I dropped on my knees next to it and poised the tip of the shovel over its throat while keeping my eyes averted. For them, I had to do it. For them. I shoved down and the shovel met resistance against its fur. My stomach lurched again and vomit crawled up my throat. I tried again and—It. Would. Not. Go. Through. Just as I'd feared.

Not that I could stomach taking its head off.

The monster grumbled. I stiffened and squeezed my eyes tightly shut. One second passed, then two. Nothing happened. It didn't attack. I peeked at the still body and breathed a sigh of relief. The glow from the interwoven strands in the fur extinguished. If I went to get Jason from the house, he would do the same thing I just tried, but I doubted he could do much against a monster. Before age had caught up to him, I would have had no doubt he'd be able to hold his own, even against this massive beast, but now? No, I wouldn't tell him. Bringing him would just put him in harm's way if the creature woke up.

I licked my lips, and the shovel thumped on the floor. I could appeal to it in a different way. After all, one thing Pam always said was that monsters were intelligent.

I chewed on my lower lip and gave in to helping it. Taking hold of its arm, I struggled to lift it to get a better look at its wounds in the candlelight. Blood dripped down my hands and I immediately set it back on the floor. Upon it thumping hard, the slight glow flared and just as quickly tamped down again.

I leaned over its throat. The fleshy pink meat of the ruptured flesh made it difficult to swallow. Even with the neck already cut open, I'd been unable to wedge the tip of the shovel deeper. This damage had been done by something much more powerful than me.

What if it was out there still? My muscles seized.

It would have found the beast and finished it off, right? Or perhaps, this one had killed the other . . .

That was what I would have to go with, I had to deal with the one at my feet.

The rhythm of its breathing changed. And was that a growl? My eyes snapped up to glowing orange eyes so bright it made my eyes water looking up at them.

I gasped and it was the trigger to send it lunging at me. I jerked back in time to avoid the monster biting off my nose.

Using my palms, I dragged myself backwards, but the monster moved faster than I could see. Claws raked across my thigh, opening up a nasty gash through my jeans. I cried out and suddenly the large clawed hand grasped onto my shoulder, forcing me down so I was flat.

Streaks of orange strands were painted within its dark fur, illuminated with a soft glow. The beast blinked blazing orange eyes, the glow growing as it huffed out breaths. A snarl left its muzzle letting me see flashes of its sharp, pointy fangs. I put my hands on its chest like I could restrain it from dipping and sliding them into my throat. It snarled again and flashed a full set of teeth. I squeezed my eyes shut. This was the end.

But no agonizing bite came. Suddenly, weight fell on top of me, exploding the breath from my lungs. I grunted under the suffocating weight. Fur pressed against my skin, oddly silky and warm against me.

It'd passed out.

A wolf-monster had passed out on top of me in the process of killing me.

I STRUGGLED TO BREATHE WITH THE WEIGHT crushing my chest. Sinking my fingers into the thick pelt, I tried shoving the monster off, but it wouldn't budge. Blood dripped onto my cheek, tickling on its way down my neck. I wriggled, trying to wrestle my arm free to dash the liquid away, but couldn't get loose. My heartbeat drummed in my ears, frantic and panicked. If I continued flailing under the beast like this, I'd run out of energy and end up a corpse via suffocation.

I stopped trying to escape. Closing my eyes, I took a few deep breaths to get myself under control. The large chest shuddered and a rumble, different from his earlier aggression, shook its chest. The sound reached out and gripped my throat. Such pain in it . . .

Now that I'd stopped thrashing, the weight wasn't as unbearable, at least not suffocating. Straightening my leg as much as it could go, I inched it over until I freed it. It let out another whimper and with the vibration, the beast shifted over, loosening the weight on my arm. With the same little movement and a wiggle to the side, I managed to get my other arm out from between its chest and mine. Fur rubbed against my exposed arms. Another move of my hips and I was free. Rolling to my side, I got to my knees as I scrambled away from the monster. It continued to breathe with loud rumbling huffs. As if it took great effort.

My thigh burned and I pressed my palm against the wounds, hissing from the sting. I turned my back to the monster and pushed my bloody palm into the wooden leg of my counter, using it to quickly push myself to my feet.

Another low, guttural sound of pain rumbled in its large chest, the sound resonating until I could feel it to my bones. The hair on my arms lifted and I whipped around, expecting it to be coming for me again, but it remained lying there, trembling.

As scared as I was, it seemed so pitiful and broken, splayed on the cold ground. Poor thing looked like it'd been sliced and roughly sewn back together.

Blood continued leaking into the ripped, jagged edges of my pants. I needed new clothes and a plan. Sitting here feeling sorry for something that had just tried to kill me would get me nowhere.

With nausea twisting my stomach, I ran from my shack. Descending the stairs hurt more than I expected, but I didn't slow in my dash through the woods. My leg wound stung with every step, and since the shack was a distance away from the house, it took me a while of trekking through the woods. I broke free of the forest, and the towering house was still quite a distance away. Red had spread into my jeans, soaking the material down to my knee.

Eventually, the creature would muster the strength to get

up, despite the severity of its injuries. And from there it would come for me . . . for us.

I'd heard stories of what monsters were capable of and how their cruelty knew no bounds. Maybe I could bargain with it?

Help it as long as it left Jason and Pam alone. They'd done so much for me by taking me in after they found me alone in the middle of the woods. I was too young to remember how or why, or maybe trauma blocked the memory from me, but either way, they were all I knew. I knew Jason and Pam would not leave their home no matter how much I begged, even if I said it was only for a little while. They were prideful people.

If I brought it food to fill its belly, maybe the wolf-like monster would not eat us?

The leaves and foliage I stepped over became dirt with patches of grass sprouting from the ground. I followed the winding path up to the front wrap around porch. Pam told me it was a colonial style home, which meant absolutely nothing to me. It had something to do with how it was built and the specific structure from decades ago, before the Rift. Or something like that. Honestly, I wasn't too sure. I wouldn't know more than what she told me since this world full of monsters was all I knew.

Each step of the stairs leading up to the door tugged at the injury on my wounded leg. I sank my teeth into my lip to hold back a whimper. I reached the landing and kicked off my tall boots to slide my feet into my indoor slippers. The metal screen door creaked, making me wince. Pam and Jason's bedroom was on the first floor, just past the kitchen, but hopefully they were deep enough asleep that they didn't hear it. Tiptoeing over the gray carpet, I crossed the thin hallway leading into the living room where the stairs went up to my room on the second floor.

I hurried past the unused bedrooms until I reached mine across the wall adorned with fruit paintings, shutting the door as quietly as possible. Once inside, I grabbed my first aid kit from under my bathroom sink and quickly discarded my jeans. I perched on the edge of my mattress only in my underwear. The gashes were still fresh, raw and bloody, but the blood that stained my skin had dried and begun to flake. Grabbing the disinfectant spray, I spritzed it over the wound. It immediately began to bubble. I hissed a breath out between my teeth, fanning my hand over it to send waves of relief over the raw, stinging flesh.

I worked on dabbing the crusted blood away and cleaned it so I could wrap it. I rolled the bandage around my thigh, tightening it until the edges snuggly hugged my leg. Once done, the white roll of cotton protected and covered the entire wound.

Wood creaked outside my room. It was that third step climbing up. I made sure not to set my weight on it if I wanted to keep quiet.

Quickly closing up my kit, I shoved it under the bed and climbed under my sheets. If Jason or Pam saw me, the questions they'd hit me with would out me. I couldn't lie even a little. I clenched the cotton of my blanket and peeked out from under my eyelashes.

The door slowly creaked open. I could hear my heartbeat pick up pace, but I worked to make my breathing normal, like I was sleeping.

Jason's wide shoulders were outlined in the entry. He stood there and I kept as still as possible. He was checking in on me.

After a few beats, he backed out and shut the door, leaving

me in a room only lit by the moon. I waited for the creak of the third step and climbed out of bed, walking directly to my closet.

Wearing leggings wouldn't be comfortable with my leg torn up like this, so I grabbed a white, knee length dress. Shucking off my shirt, I slipped it on.

I'd collect food and some things to clean up its wounds before sneaking out again.

The creature was hurt, and even though it almost ate me, I had to try to save all of us.

I BALANCED THE WARM POT OF FOOD ON TOP OF THE medium-sized bucket containing towels soaking in warm water. I'd brought leftover boiled chicken on a bed of rice in hopes that it would help garner its favor. Heat seeped through the plastic, warming my torso and making the bite of cold night air not so harsh.

The chickens from the coop chirped at me accusingly as I passed. Pam had Jason and me build it this far away because she hated all the noise in the morning.

It didn't take me terribly long to get to my destination. My path was practically embedded into the forest floor from how often I walked it.

I slowed as I approached the shack door. My stomach churned. Would it kill me as soon as it could? Would it allow me a moment to plead my case? I'd never felt more like throwing up. I sucked in a deep breath as I climbed up the steps. The hollow thuds echoed too loudly. Crows cawed above my head. I wet my lips and entered.

The monster lay in the same position as when I left,

breathing so harshly its shoulders jerked and the intimidating buck-like antlers gouged the wooden floor. I'd rushed out earlier and hadn't even blown out the candle.

Gently setting down the materials I'd brought, I slowly approached. I debated grabbing the discarded shovel that had landed somewhere under the table, but it'd be stupid. The creature could rip my heart out before I could get to it and even if I did, I wouldn't be able to kill it.

With a calm mind, I inspected the wounds. The gashes looked awful. My stomach ached and I forced my gaze to the rest of the beast. Its muzzle and nose were coated in slicing cuts, and the same injuries were littered throughout the massive body, gnarly wide ones that had split his blood-orange tissue.

Shredded flesh scattered throughout its fur leaked inky liquid. I grimaced. What had done this? My stomach dropped to my feet. My breaths puffed from my mouth exaggeratedly. Everything was okay. It would be fine and was fine. I let out a long breath through puckered lips.

I padded over to where I'd left my things, set the food aside and collected the warm bucket to bring it closer. The container thumped a little harder on the floor than I meant it to and I froze, sucking in a breath. The monster didn't move. I popped the top and a waft of steam seeped out, the drenched hand towels floated in the shallow water.

Grabbing one, I crouched in front of the wolf-monster and began swiping at the blood trickling into its eyes. My hand trembled with each motion, but I couldn't stave it off. I wasn't stupid, my life hung in the balance, but I had to try.

It breathed in harshly, its entire body shuddering . . . its eyes popped opened, the glow of them almost blinding me. In a sudden burst, the beast had me flat on the ground again, my back thumping down hard. A scream wrenched free, but I thinned my lips. I squeezed my eyes shut, turning my head to the side to expose my throat.

"I was trying to help you," I breathed, my voice verging on a whimper. "Please. I just want to make a deal. Please."

Only silence. Its nose no longer grazed along my exposed throat, but its claws continued to dig into my chest.

"A deal." I could taste his derision. The voice was gravely and deep, unmistakably male. "I do not make deals with humans. You are unworthy of even our presence." I peeked up at him and the inhuman eyes stared at me unsympathetically. I didn't know how to explain it, but it felt like evil stared back at me.

"I brought food for you—"

"You try to poison me?" He hissed.

"No." I pushed the word through my tight esophagus. I shook my head hard. "Please. I will help you. I can bring you anything you need and cook for you. You need to heal, right? Because of how weak you are—"

He snarled.

He did not like that.

"I swear to do whatever you say, you won't get any opposition from me."

I was blabbing at this point, but I kept spitting things out until something stuck with him, until he agreed to what I wanted.

"I just want one thing—"

Canines glinted with his sneer. I swallowed my scream.

"Leave my family alone. That's it. You can even eat me if you want." My voice warbled. To the one thing I feared saying, he finally looked intrigued. His orange eyes flared with light, causing my stomach to sour. The building tears spilled from the corner of my eyes in rivulets. "I won't try to escape you."

The beast's head tilted to the side without expression. I didn't think he *could* have an expression. Teeth bared at me, the extra, extra large incisors at the top and bottom of his muzzle slicing fear through my heart.

The light from the glowing strands of fur and eyes blazed bright and glinted off those sharp canine fangs. They came down at me . . . and a tongue flicked out to drag across my eyes.

I went rigid.

The wet, long, and velvety tongue collected the droplets, but they continued spilling through my scrunched eyes.

It felt . . . soothing? I curled my fingers, trying to keep my hands to myself when all I wanted to do was shove him back. This felt too odd, not natural but I forced myself to stay still, to prove to him that I would keep my word and let him do what he wanted to me. Even if it meant my death.

WHY WAS SHE LEAKING FROM HER FACE? WHAT SMELL was this? I flared my nose as I tasted the water coming from her eyes.

The taste spread on my tongue and a shiver coasted down my spine to my tail. I shook my fur. Even the agony of my cuts did nothing to take away from the pleasure the taste of her liquid gave me.

I lapped her face, collecting the moisture tracing down her small, flat muzzle. She did not move under me, keeping still as if knowing I would rip her throat out if she twitched. After collecting the rest of the moisture with my tongue, it stopped coming.

"More," I snarled. She startled, a harsh breath exploding from the fleshiness framing her blunt teeth. I sniffed and dipped my head to follow the deliciousness.

There was more of the taste here. I slid my tongue inside her odd human muzzle, licking and tasting her. I didn't understand this moisture she leaked, but she tasted delicious. Like the crisp woods I had smelled when I escaped the torment of my captivity.

She made a sound, and it vibrated against my tongue. Her little hands gripped my horning.

I stiffened, baring my teeth in her face. She flinched and let me go, cowering below me. Such a small human. All humans were nothing compared to my size, but this one seemed smaller than the ones I had encountered. I curled my lip at the thought of them. Unlike any I had seen, she held extra flesh in her legs and midsection. I could never understand how they survived with such weak, fragile bodies. Not even fur protected them. Preposterous.

Humans were nothing in a fight against a creature, and I'd eaten my fair share of them. I did not need her acceptance to feed on her flesh, but my injuries weakened me, and I did not want to expose myself to another fight. I would not risk capture.

My captivity began so long ago . . . if I hadn't been weakened by my fight with the pack of Arbols, those humans would have never caught me as a youngling.

I had not been slain, instead, I'd woken chained and bleeding on a table.

They'd sliced through my gut and torso multiple times. I watched in agony as they rifled through my insides and then stitched me up—too many times to count. Used for *scientific* reasons, I'd heard them say. I flexed my claws, slicing the ground.

If I did not heal quickly, I could not reign destruction upon them as they deserved. I wanted to do it soon.

I sneered and the girl flinched, her arms wrapped around her torso, over the plump extra flesh—the bits that female humans had. This one had an excess from what I had seen of the others.

I lowered my muzzle and tasted her neck with slow, gliding laps. Her death was calling. I'd sink my teeth into her and feed on her entrails.

It would not be enough to immediately garner strength, but —my nose twitched. A tantalizing scent curled to my nose.

A succulence I had only ever scented on her invaded my senses. Where was it coming from? I breathed in deeper, following it. Lower and lower until I pressed my nose between her hind legs.

Here. I inhaled deeper, sucking in the sweetness perfuming off her skin. Causing a hunger so violent it caused my cock to twitch within my slit.

A growl vibrated my diaphragm, and I sniffed her into my lungs.

"What are you doing?" She squealed in a high-pitched voice, grating on my ears. I flicked them to rid the irritation and shoved my nose harder against the warmth between her legs. She jolted as if I'd struck my claws into her throat. I would devour this smell, claim it, own it until the female died. I would begin my feast here.

She gripped my horning again and I snarled in warning. She let go hastily, thumping onto her back, staring down at me with wide eyes. My glow cast over her features.

I delved under the fabric covering what I wanted, and fortunately, the weak, thin skin of her legs was already bare to me. Another tight fabric covered the scent, and I snarled. Her legs trembled as I opened my maw over the covered flesh between her legs.

"W-what are you doing? Those are my underwea—" I

yanked the fabric. The taste of blood coated my tongue, and she screeched. A thin line bled from my fang catching the flesh above the area I sought.

Upon her being bared, the potency of her scent hit me. I groaned gutturally. The fur on my back stood and a shiver coasted down my spine. I lowered my head, needing to get closer, but her legs slammed together.

"Do not hide it from me," I snarled.

"But you're sniffing my sex," she whispered. Her eyes were large, like they could take up half her face. Humans were odd looking creatures. The soft, flat muzzles, the bare fur-less flesh, ugly things.

I snarled.

Her small body jolted, and her knees slowly opened, revealing, pink, damp flesh below a tuft of fur. The flesh looked unlike anything I had ever seen. It throbbed. It was hypnotizing.

This was her *sex*, where she reproduced with the males of her species . . . and like my species—lycans, as the humans referred to us—also had their sexual organs at the apex of their legs.

I'd assumed it was humans' muzzles that birthed young since I had seen them taste monsters' sexual areas to harvest the potent liquid from our release.

The female humans I overheard described our organs as 'cocks'. They seemed gleeful at having a taste, but breeding was purely for reproducing, they should not be taking joy from it.

I had not been one of the subjects used this way, the *scientists* preferred to rip me into shreds to see what I could survive.

She yelped upon my nose touching her, her legs trembling. I

bared my teeth in warning, and she kept her legs spread. Her wide eyes rounded and her face turned pink.

Humans were a strange, unattractive breed, but then why did this one look so . . . soft.

Upon my tongue lapping across her, her small hands pressed over her muzzle, but a soft whine escaped.

A potent sweet taste unlike anything I had eaten shocked my system. My cock emerged from its slit, engorged and twitching. So large it pressed against the human's leg. She tensed, but I didn't allow another second to pass.

I repeated the same lick. Her slick coated my tongue and a shiver lifted the fur on my body.

Unmatched delicacy.

I trembled, lashing my tongue into the tightness of the petals and it gave way, allowing me to plunge into a channel to seek more of her taste. Her inner walls squeezed my tongue, and her hips frantically moved.

The more I licked, the more liquid she offered my tongue. With each gush and flick, she offered me needy whimpers. I wanted this pleasure and taste drawn out.

She would not die. She would be owned by me. Do as I ordered until I tired of her or until I gathered my strength to seek vengeance against the vile humans who took pleasure in slicing sharp objects into my body in the name of 'discovery'— whichever came first.

I slid my tongue up the sides of her leaking crevices, gyrating forward until the tip of my member pressed into her leg. I flicked my tongue deeper into her and her body tensed, her small muzzle opening. She cried out, the call wild and visceral, forcing a growl from my throat and causing my cock to throb.

She jackknifed her hips up and her channel squeezed my tongue. Her shout now mingled with whimpers.

My hips continued to pump against the slightest touch of her leg, my knot swelling in preparation for release. A tremor worked up my spine. A foreign sensation built in my gut, and warmth spread down. What was happening to me? I could not contain myself. Slamming my claws on the ground, I raked them into the wood, gouging into the surface.

My sack drew tight and gut-wrenching pleasure webbed through every inch of my limbs, turning them useless. In a sudden burst, I could no longer breathe, and heat exploded from the tip of my cock in a gush. A guttural sound roared from my chest. Glowing release splattered over the human's legs and onto the fabric covering her.

I swayed forward, my injuries throbbing from the grind of my hips. Weakness I would not allow while being around a human. Shaking my head to rid the drag on my limbs begging me to drop to unconsciousness, I bent to lick my release from her legs, cleaning her with quick, swift swipes. She gasped with each lave of my tongue.

I had never released. When lycan's mated, the females dug their claws into the male and did not release the male they selected. Before my captivity, I had kept my distance in order to not be bound to a female. That choice had not changed. But this was a human, to use and discard.

I sat back on my haunches, my cock still throbbing with need. My release painted the sides of the thick pulsating member.

Her eyes fastened upon it. A high-pitched scream speared my ears. Her already small eyes became even larger.

"What is that? I-I mean, I know what it is in theory, b-but . . ."

I bared my teeth proudly.

"Clean me off, human." The words flowed too easily. I did not enjoy touch, any touch, regardless of species, but even more so from humans. They were disgusting and weak, but this one smelled so enticing.

She closed and opened her eyes quickly.

"Y-you want me to lick your cum?" There was a tilt to the end of her words, but I could not understand what was difficult about my order. Irritation washed away my confusion.

"Now." I sneered. I cocked my head, watching the plump, fur-less human jolt as if she would flee. I would rip her head off if she attempted it. I cocked my head, watching the human's next move. What would she do?

Her human muzzle thinned, and she bent forward until she crawled the distance separating us. Her clothing fell forward and covered her sweet taste. A growl vibrated in my throat. I swayed forward to slice my claws through the offending fabric blocking her heat. The room tipped and I slammed my claws on the ground to steady my body before I fell to the side. A frustrated huff left my muzzle.

She settled before me, her gaze fastened on the tip of my breeding member where my luminescent need awaited her. Her hands wrapped around my flesh, above my knot, and she gasped, flexing her fingers against my shaft. I grunted, my glow flaring bright until it illuminated her. It took both her hands to grip my width. Her touch was hesitant—gentle. Unlike any other touch I had ever felt upon me. Panting came through my clenched teeth.

Her small tongue poked out across the plush flesh of her

human muzzle. She leaned forward and gingerly flicked her tongue out again, collecting my seed.

I groaned, my hips bucking up. This-I-Such pleasure. How delicious. Why did her tongue feel this way? Her eyes flicked up. She licked me again, sending ecstasy through my veins.

"More." I snarled and buried my claws into her hair to force her muzzle flush to my throbbing tip, my hips bucking desperately. A guttural sound I'd never made before rumbled from my muzzle—then she slid both hands down, taking the pleasure to the base of my cock where my knot waited.

I couldn't take this fascinating pleasure—

AND FOR THE SECOND TIME, I FOUND MYSELF smushed under the large unconscious monster. One second, I was rubbing my palms down the biggest cock I could have never imagined, the next, I was flat on the ground with the wolf-monster on top of me. A confirmed, incredibly *male* wolf-monster. I could already tell from his voice, but this was . . . different.

Heat infused my face like it could melt it off. His large, heavy arm pinned me to the ground by my stomach. I stared at the roof of the shack, panting—stunned.

Even with the lack of contact I had with other humans, I had Pam's erotic novels, so I understood the concept of sex and all the mechanics of it even if I'd never participated—but goodness gracious. As wrong as it was, and I knew it was wrong, it felt so good when he licked me. Even the prick of his claws pressing into my flesh felt good. I closed my eyes, breathing out slowly.

A madness had come over me and I hadn't stopped moving under his tongue. God help me, I'd wanted more. Even his cum tasted good, which I had not expected of the glowing orange substance. Nor had I expected the tingling sensation when his cum touched my tongue. Or how warmth spread through my insides as soon as I swallowed. Like I'd slipped into a hot bath.

The feel of his cock remained imprinted on my hands, the slippery, wet member throbbing against my touch, while the faint indent of veins pulsed.

I squeezed my eyes tight, fisting my hands against the wood floors. My heartbeat hadn't calmed down and I doubted it would until I was far away from this creature. His arm remained across my midsection, pinning me down. He'd never responded to my proposal, and if I wasn't mistaken, he had found it funny when I asked. I rolled the back of my head against the wooden floors. If I went back home and told them about all of this, they would refuse to flee, and even worse, Jason would come out here to shoot him even if he well knew bullets didn't kill monsters. No, telling Jason would lead to his death.

I pushed to my elbows and his powerful growl vibrated the floor. His large head moved and one of his antlers almost poked one of my eyes out. I flinched, studying the bone bursting outward from the top of his head. His furred pointy ears flicked side to side. Heat radiated from his body. Sweltering warmth that dug under my skin, making the chilled room warm.

I moved an inch to the side but his thick arm curved tight around me, dragging me closer. I gasped at the suddenness. My side was flush to his, his arm securing me close. Guarding me like a dog with a bone. The movement dragged my dress higher until the ground abrasively rubbed against my bare skin.

He nestled me against his wide chest, his arm curved across my stomach and breasts in a diagonal. The double-jointed section at the wrist area curved under my side boob. His hand—

paw, or whatever it was called, felt odd. They looked like overgrown human fingers but much longer than normal, and a thin layer of rough flesh coated only the fingertips while silky fur covered the rest. Claws tipped the top of them, slightly curling at the ends. One of them currently dug into the soft side of my boob. With one twitch he'd pierce my skin.

He was frighteningly large, from top to bottom and everywhere in between.

I wet my lip. What to do? His fur felt amazingly silky and long against my bare skin . . . I wiggled under his arm again and my movement caused his dimmed glow to catch on something glistening in his fur. A gash across his wrist. Part of his skin was flayed off.

His fur was smoothed in patches across his body and upon further inspection, I could make out the ridges of unhealed flesh crusted with a dried, dark substance. One started at the side of his neck and disappeared under his body. I squinted with the minimal lighting, trying to get a better look, but the position of his body didn't allow it.

A slice across his snout leaked very faintly. I hadn't noticed it was blood until now because his dark fur camouflaged it. The circular injury looked like a muzzle had been clipped onto his face, begun to grow into his skin and then been ripped off.

My goodness, what had been done to this creature?

Despite myself, sympathy crawled into my heart. All of these injuries at this level were cruel. I wiggled a little higher and stopped. When he didn't move, I kept moving higher until I managed to sit on my butt, and his arm squeezed around my thigh. Even though fur covered his arm, I could see the dip of the muscle in his arm. The thick cording twitched against my legs, making me seem tiny next to his size.

I reached for the bucket I'd left on the ground and inched it over with little dragging tugs until I had it next to me. Water sloshed over the lip and seeped through the wood slats.

Reaching inside the tepid water, I grabbed the remaining drenched cloth and wrung it out. Bringing the damp towel over, I swiped it across his muzzle, cleaning off the crusted injury as best as I could.

He twitched and a disturbed half-huff, half-growl rumbled in his throat. He still didn't wake, so I set to work, making my way toward his eye where he had similar cuts and to his ear which looked like it had almost been snipped vertically.

I was concentrating entirely on swiping the now-stained rag against the base of his antlers where there were deep gouges when the arm around me stiffened.

From one breath to the next a snarl, so violent and spine tingling, exploded from his chest. He jerked his claws back so fast that they sliced into my leg again. Stabbing agony ripped through my thigh, taking my breath away. When I could suck breath into my lungs, I whimpered.

"Do not touch me unless I order it of you."

My voice stuck in my throat as my brain went into flight and I started to drag myself backwards, my limp, agonized leg leaving a trail of blood. He snarled again and I stopped moving.

I watched him with bated breath. His head had lowered as he eyed me menacingly, looking on the verge of pouncing. He panted; fur lifting on the back of his neck, his eyes glowing brightly to the point that it hurt to look at him.

His large, white teeth were bared, and he hadn't moved. He regarded me without expression, and I couldn't help but feel his derision.

Tears streamed down my cheeks and dripped off my chin.

Still, he just watched me as if he were about to tear out my throat. This was it for me. Once I was dead, Pam and Jason would be next.

My throat closed to the point that it hurt to breathe. At least I wouldn't live to see my family killed.

"I-I was just trying to help you." Words tumbled free, half-hiccupped from my crying. My leg burned so badly.

I clasped the top of my thigh with a wince. There was no sight of the bandage I'd wrapped around my leg earlier, so the scratches were exposed. The ripped fabric must have landed in some dark corner of the shack. Thin lines . . . maybe the cuts weren't as deep as I thought.

He rose to his hind legs, looming over me until his antlers touched the ceiling. His body curved forward because of the joint at his foot that elongated and stretched to give him the agility to be on all fours and to straighten bipedally with ease. In two wide steps he was in my face.

I squeezed my eyes tight. His warm breath fluttered my hair back . . .

SIX

FENRIR

I COCKED MY HEAD, STUDYING THE FLINCHING human. A scent emitted from her and burned my nose with each inhale. I sneezed to rid myself of the smell. Bitterness mingled with the sweet scent she carried. Human fear had a distinct scent, but unlike the revelry I felt in smelling other human's fear, hers burned.

She breathed harshly. Her leg gushed blood. I could easily rip her head off and feast on her flesh. I'd done it plenty of times and this one had done much worse than the ones I'd devoured.

How dare she touch me without my allowing it?

I licked my incisors as I dropped to all fours. Such a small human, I could swallow her in two bites.

I breathed out, and the fur atop her head fluttered around her strange face. Still, she remained unmoving and trembling, her eyes shut until little furrows appeared. The liquid dripping off her face caused my hunger to swell.

I opened my maw, twisting my head to envelop her throat. A small whimper fell from her. I could end her now, and gain strength to find more meals. All I had to do was sink my teeth into her and hear the satisfying pop of her skin giving way. Another of her weak sounds assaulted my ears and I snarled, backing away from her.

"Silence."

She jolted.

The ones that I had been exposed to did not cause me to hunger this way.

If I devoured her . . . I would no longer have the sweet taste between her legs, or even the one leaking from her face.

I would never find it again once I tore her head off.

A growl vibrated my chest. I succumbed to the urge to run my tongue across her face to take the wet from her eyes. I ignored her gasp.

I cocked my head. Why would I want to lick it off? Clean her like she was my cub . . . no, as if she were my female? I sniffed her.

A visceral need throbbed through my cock. I breathed her in again, burying my muzzle into her neck. An urge to rut her gripped my cock. Heaviness collected down at my slit. My hidden sex throbbed, growing from the apex of my thighs. It emerged from my slit, ready and hard for her. The glistening member expanded until it was painfully hard, throbbing, and leaking at the tip.

She pulled this reaction of my cock only from a thought. I loomed over her, preparing to use her to sate these newfound rutting urges.

She flinched back and her expression scrunched as a sharp yelp slipped free of her small muzzle.

In pain?

She cradled her leg, curling forward. Akin to a wounded

creature protecting themselves. I reached for her human paw and pulled it up to see what she hid.

She screamed, but it was easy to ignore. Blood dripped to the floor and puddled under her. The bottom of the ripped cloth she wore had become stained in bright human blood. Too much for her to survive if it continued. The human would not last long with her life blood leaking from her.

I knew well—if she had not taken the little of my release that she did, she would no longer have a limb. If she swallowed more, she would have no injury.

I would not allow her to die. Not yet.

"You will feed from me."

Her small face turned up toward me.

"F-feed?"

I cupped the back of her neck, my paw wrapping fully around her throat to pull her up easily. She yelped and scrambled to get her weak legs under her.

"I will protect you." I clicked my teeth in her face. She scrunched her eyes closed.

I had offered her my protection as my pet human, and she did not fall at my feet in gratitude?

Any lycan female would have presented themselves to me already.

With a hard grip, I yanked her closer. She had no ability to escape, she was too weak. Her eyes widened . . . the sour scent of fear threatened to overwhelm me.

I slammed onto all fours, leaning over her face.

"Do not fear me," I snarled.

She sucked in a breath, flat face tilting up to stare at me. A wash of my glow fell over her, illuminating the dampness beneath her eyes. Leaning down, I swiped my tongue across the liquid to collect the drops.

She jerked and blinked once.

The bitterness of her fear faded, replaced by the smell I enjoyed. Rising to my hind legs, I presented my member to her small muzzle. I curled my claws into the fur on her head, guiding her forward. The plush flesh where she spoke from, her human muzzle, parted and spread over the leaking tip. A guttural whine ripped from my chest.

"Do not remove your muzzle," I ordered.

A small line formed between the fur above her eyes and she pulled away from my member despite my command.

"It's called my mouth." The corner of her *mouth* twitched down.

"Continue," I growled, forcing her back onto my tip. She opened up, taking the thick head inside. My cock pulsated. Her warm tongue flicked against my flesh. I bared my teeth.

Her paws lifted, wrapping around my veined, damp thickness. When she rubbed them down to the base of my knot, it drove my hips forward. She stopped and rolled her touch over my knot again.

Hunger wove through my gut. Nothing had ever felt so delicious.

A purr vibrated my chest—then she rubbed down my slickness, sending fire blazing through my gut.

Madness gripped me and my hips bucked, trying to get more of her mouth. Her touch slipped down my member, wrapping around the base. They spread wide from necessity since her paws were much too small. She rubbed it in little movements that caused whimpers to spill from my maw.

I couldn't contain myself. Sounds spilled from behind

gritted teeth, but instead of stopping, my pleasure bolstered her movements. Fire exploded out and manifested in my release.

Curving forward, my body jerked with each liquid jut of release. So much that it spilled from her mouth and trickled off her jaw.

She made another noise I had never heard from a human. She enjoyed my taste? I no longer gripped her head, and still she lapped my leaking tip like it was her last meal. Her small hands bunched my fur next to my cock slit, and the tug caused a wave of pleasure.

She undid me. My knot throbbed. I should have taken her and locked my cock inside her. Another wave of release painted her chest. The last one. Shuddering, I stumbled back, panting, unable to remain steady.

She fell forward onto all fours, the long fur on her head falling into her face. I wanted more—and to be inside her, to force her to take all of me—

I shook my head, my horning scraping against the wall. Exhaustion weighed my limbs down. Rest first and then I would rut her all I wanted.

I swayed, the pressure in my spine abated and my cock returned to my slit. I dropped to all fours as she remained bent over, watching me with her mouth parted and her shoulders jerking up and down. She panted as if in fear, but she did not run, or smell of fear, only the delicious sweetness emanated from between her legs, seemingly emphasized.

The injury on her leg no longer leaked blood. That was what I wanted, to keep her alive until I did not have need of her.

I hooked my paw around her side and dragged her to my torso, enfolding her to me with her spine to my abdomen.

"Do not touch me lest I order it." She grunted, and I took

the sound as assent. I had always been averse to touch, even from before, with my kin. She was a human . . . a nothing. This temptation she posed was born of necessity and madness.

"But you're touching me." Her voice was low. I could not decipher her tone, but it caused my claws to flex.

"You cannot leave." I would touch her as much as I pleased, but she did not have free rein. I pulled her much closer until I had every inch of her plastered to me. If she moved, I would feel it.

Not being constantly ripped to pieces or dissected had already offered me more strength than I had since before my capture. I simply needed rest and I would regain my true self. Once I was well enough, I would hunt and slaughter.

"What—"

"Silence, human," I growled.

"My name is Mia," she mumbled.

Mia.

"You may address me as Fenrir."

The name *they* had given me. The name I vowed never to forget.

I WIGGLED CLOSER TO THE WARMTH AT MY BACK AND rubbed my cheek against the fur I laid upon. I'd never slept so warmly or comfortably . . .

I clawed out of sleep and stiffened. I'd passed out soon after he'd tugged me to his chest with my belly warm and oddly full. Fenrir . . . the wolf-monster.

He had a name.

Somehow, it made my desire feel less wrong, when it really shouldn't have. This was for Pam and Jason . . . I didn't *want* to lick his monstrous, slick, pink cock. I swallowed with difficulty. I also shouldn't have enjoyed it as much as I had. Even now, I felt extra sensitive between my legs—achy.

He'd acted like him feeding me his cum was a gift—not meant to be sexual, but the interaction was still charged with tension. And as sick as it was, I wanted more. His taste had tingled on my tongue, oddly delicious for glowing cum. He kind of tasted fruity. Closer to strawberries and oranges.

I ran my palm down his arm, encountering matted fur. I worked my fingers through it as gently as possible. A low hum turned into vibrations against my back. Underneath the thick fur was raised skin. I nestled my fingers through it to see what it was and saw brown skin under the fur. The flesh was scarred, like barbed wreaths had been twined around his arms and then he'd been dragged by it. The wounds must have been awful for them to have healed this way.

What happened to him?

His oversized muzzle nuzzled into the crook of my neck. His throat settled over my ear, causing the purring to turn into a roar. His pine scent enveloped me, overwhelming most of the bitter copper scent as I breathed. Nestling against him shouldn't make me feel all warm and fuzzy inside. I continued combing the spot with my fingers.

Bits of dried blood flaked off, and without it so matted, his fur was just as silky as it was by his legs. The unfamiliar texture was oddly alluring. I scratched his skin. The low rumble turned up multiple notches. How fascinating.

Suddenly, the sounds against my ear shut off and he stiffened. With a jerky movement, he yanked away. My ear, formerly nestled against his comfortable arm, smacked against the floorboard.

I yelped and huddled into a ball, shutting off my sight. Claws poked my shoulder and then his palm flattened against it. He jerked me to roll over toward him.

"Why are you behaving this way?" He extended his claw toward my lips, the sharp tip piercing the lower one. He pinched my dress between his claws and lifted me. The collar of my dress dug into my throat and the frayed hem tickled my thighs. I winced.

"You scared me." I wheezed the words, dangling from his grip like a rag.

"Fear." He grunted. "But uninjured." He seemed to be speaking to himself. He gently lowered me until he was no longer grabbing my clothes. His glowing gaze refocused on my face; the shine so bright I had to drop my attention to his sharp teeth.

His large head bowed down to hover close and his long, warm tongue lashed across both my lips. I gasped, and part of his tongue flicked inside my mouth and then across my scratched lip.

His glow flared again, and he straightened over me.

"You were ordered not to touch." The force of his words made me want to drop my eyes.

I needed to stop setting the monster off. Making him angry would get me nowhere.

"I'm sorry. I was trying to get the tangles out of your fur." I peeked up at him and he watched me with his head tilted. "Who hurt you? You have dried blood matted to your body. Is that why you're so aggressive? I was just trying to help . . ."

I trailed off and cleared my throat. He continued to stare at me. His gaze dimmed.

It was obvious he'd been hurt, and with how cautious he'd been, I could only draw to the conclusion that *someone* had been hurting him—for a while. It wasn't some random fight, the wounds shouted captivity. Sympathy surged forward. The monster had been reacting from pain. I scanned the matted fur again.

"Do you want to bathe?"

His head tilted.

"You know, water . . ." I waved my hands around like I was cleaning my body. There was a lake nearby that I took dips in often.

"Fenrir?"

He continued staring at me and I would have thought he hadn't heard me if the orange in his eyes didn't flare brightly at my words.

My empathy would do me in. Now that I had built up this back story for him, I couldn't help but warm to him. He cringed away from my touch but was it because he'd only ever been hurt?

The thought of this prideful, large male, fearful of touch caused my stomach to sour. I had no doubt he hated humans and thought them beneath him, but there was more here. I could show him we were not all that bad. Maybe then he wouldn't attempt to kill us.

"I won't touch you anymore," I said, giving in. "I am sorry." I slightly bowed my head like I'd seen him do. His head cocked. "I'll take you to the lake?" I posed it more as a question and took one step toward the door. When he didn't smack me down or drag me to him, I took another. Then another, keeping my eyes on him as I sidled to the door. He could easily stop me, I had no doubts about that.

The door had never shut properly, so all it needed was a nudge. The sun hung low, casting an orange light across the forest. I worked to keep my attention averted from the path leading back home. I would need to get back eventually, otherwise Jason would come seek me out. Sometimes we went days without seeing each other during harvest season, but I didn't want to chance it. If I continued to be gone, they could grow curious as to why. But I had some time, especially since Jason saw me in bed last night.

At least I was pretty sure it was last night.

Inching out the door, I peeked over my shoulder where

Fenrir loomed right behind me. I shuddered. The beast was much too quiet for his size.

"Lead," he grunted, following so close that he stepped on the back of my shoe multiple times. I stumbled forward and worked to smooth the frustration off my face. Tension radiated off him and the hair on the back of his neck was raised all the way down to his long puffy tail.

"It's not far."

"*Lead,*" he said again in a forceful, biting tone.

I scowled and picked up speed, following the grooves I'd walked into the dirt. The path ran north of the property and led toward a lake. That was as far as I'd ever gone from the house and our land. I never dared step away from my haven and I never would. I relied on the safety my home provided. I could only attribute this single-minded desire to leftover trauma from when I was a kid.

All I remembered before Pam and Jason found me was the gut-wrenching feeling of being lost. Of not knowing where to go. Of sleeping on the ground, of starving. I wasn't sure how long I'd been out here, but Pam told me I'd been *as dirty and thin as a dog,* her words.

Pam was good people, she talked with me, shared stories of how life was before the catastrophic earthquake that tore the *Rift* into the earth and ripped a new dimension through the west coast. The very reason for the monsters ending up here.

A familiar tall tree came within view, the wide branches reaching out to the sides. A bush with bright pink flowers scattered throughout the green leaves decorated the base. Cricket chirps became louder and the lake came within view, spanning until the other embankment.

"We're here," I said, more to fill the silence than anything else since it was quite clear we'd arrived.

Without waiting, he grunted and trotted forward on all fours. He submerged himself in the water until only his antlers poked above the water.

I settled myself on a flat stone near the edge of the water. As distracted as he seemed, I wasn't fooled, he'd pluck me back in place if I tried to run. Lose all the progress we'd made? No, thanks, plus I didn't want to test his strength.

I curled my legs under me, watching the monster rise from the water like some aquatic wolf god. Rivulets trickled off his slicked fur that seemed to hold a gallon of water—he was just so large. Even wet, his size didn't diminish, the fur plastered to his body, outlining the hard indents of his arms . . . and the ones at his abs. With him all wet like this, his build looked more humanoid.

Lower down, there was a slightly rounded aspect beneath the slightly bulging pouch where his cock expanded from. His balls blended with his fur.

As he stepped out, pebbles grated against each other under his weight. He left deep indents of his long double-jointed legs. The limb was different than the two arms, or front legs—depending on how I wanted to think about it. Claws erupted from their tips, hooking into the earth. Steam rose from his fur like he burned too warm for the water to remain long. He shook himself and water went flying all over the place. Splatters hit my face, sending me into a sputtering fit.

He released a collection of deep, rumbling chuffs, showing way too many teeth. If I wasn't wrong, he seemed to think it was funny.

"Jerk," I mumbled, rubbing the water off my cheek.

He dropped to all fours and shook again, sending more at me. I shielded my face, waiting until he stopped. "Now you're doing it on purpose," I muttered, scraping my hair back.

Fenrir climbed higher onto the embankment with wide, loping strides. No longer were his movements hindered by weakness. The monster had regained his strength faster than I could have imagined.

Something moved behind him, but his body blocked my sight. The small glimpse I'd seen had still been enough to see a very recognizable pelt. I jumped to my feet.

"Fenrir!" I gasped, fear vicing around my throat.

EIGHT

MIA

EVERYTHING HAPPENED WITHIN THE SPAN OF A BLINK of an eye.

I shoved off the stone, dashing toward him on instinct. I waved my hands, trying to articulate that he was being stalked by a pack of mountain lions. All our noise must have attracted them to us.

When I was alone, I took extra care to keep silent and they had never found me. I'd always been cautious because they hunted in groups, running their prey to the ground with ease. Pam said their method of hunting didn't used to be in groups. Another thing the Rift changed.

He caught me with one large claw, wrapping it around my throat and shoulder. The tip of his talon pinched my collarbone. His glowing eyes flared even brighter and his muzzle lifted to show teeth. I could only gawk up at him, frozen with fear.

"You dare attack me?" he bellowed, a rough, deadly snarl accompanying his words.

"No," I croaked, shaking my head hard. "Behind—"

One of the animals lunged at his back, sinking its teeth into his shoulder and holding on with a spine-tingling snarl.

He shoved me aside, sending me to the ground with a sharp burst of agony. My knee slammed into the hard pebbles, followed by my side. Stabs of pain shot up my hip and wrenched a gasp from my throat.

The mountain lion's yowl was muffled as it shook his head to bury its teeth deeper into Fenrir's shoulder.

Fenrir released a loud huff . . . as if exasperated. Calmly, too calmly, he reached back, gripped the scruff of the mountain lion's neck and yanked it off. Skin and fur tore, but he didn't even wince. The feline's mouth dripped onyx blood across the ground as Fenrir swung it in front of him.

It was like a fly to a human. He held the animal's feet off the ground, intelligent eyes studying the thrashing creature struggling for freedom.

In a smooth motion, he tore the lion in half. Blood spattered across my face. Guts and more unrecognizable innards dangled from both halves of the lion.

I screamed, dragging myself backward with my heels. Bile rose in my throat and the only reason it hadn't exited was because I couldn't stop screaming. He dropped onto all fours, his face splattered with bright red lion blood.

"Silence." He snarled at me. I choked on my next inhale and clamped my lips shut.

The other lion lunged, and he caught it midair, his large oddly jointed hand around its throat. The big cat sank its claws into his arm, clinging with desperation, but a crunch later and it went limp. He let it go and it dropped to the ground with a thump. The monster prowled toward his prey, blood-splattered nose audibly sniffing.

Fenrir sank his teeth into the animal he'd torn in half, eating with large bites. Bones snapped and the nauseating sounds of eating ensued. I averted my eyes.

Better the lion than me?

I breathed in and out through my nose, trying to ignore the bile clenching my stomach. Those mountain lions were nothing to him, to the point that it was sad.

I shakily stood and limped to the lake. Crouching over the edge, I splashed water on my face. He'd swatted me away so easily that it shocked me that he hadn't shattered any of my bones.

I gingerly settled on the hard ground with my legs crossed. I leaned forward, staring at the murky water. The last remnants of the sunset reflected off the surface. I'd never stayed out here this late, it looked almost magical. Slipping my hand into the shallow end, I swished it around in the cold water. When the sun was highest in the sky was the best time to get in because it wasn't *this* cold. My fingers quickly became numb and a shiver worked down my spine. My body woke up from the shock of watching Fenrir rip the lions apart. I closed my eyes and sat, breathing in deep breaths.

The bone crunching lasted a while. It was clear now more than ever that he'd been gentle with me so far. He'd obliterated those mountain lions as easily as breathing.

What had been strong enough to put him in the state I'd found him? I hugged myself. I didn't want to think about it.

With the disappearance of the sun, the weather incrementally cooled. I tucked my hands into my armpits, staring across the still surface of the water and watching the moon rise in its reflection.

His sounds of feeding tapered off. Dry shrubbery crunched and his stature blocked the moonlight. I slowly looked over my shoulder. If not for his glowing eyes and the matching tufts of fur, he would have blended with the darkness.

"You have not fed." His words were muffled, then something thumped next to my leg. An intact leg ripped out from the hip. The meaty flesh glinted orange from his glow. My stomach lurched and I clamped my hand over my mouth.

I gawked up at him, horrified. He seemed so serious. I struggled to swallow and cleared my throat.

"Oh, how nice . . ." I swallowed down the nausea. "But no thanks."

His head tilted.

"Feed," he repeated, a low, frightening rumble in his order.

"No," I said with more force. He bared his teeth and dropped to all fours, his large muzzle nearing my face. I huddled into myself. As much as he would order, I refused to eat the raw flesh. I pressed my lips into a thin line.

A disgruntled noise rumbled in his throat.

"Suit yourself." He easily broke the limb apart. I looked away before I got the gory sight of him devouring it.

As soon as the crunching ceased, I peeked up at him licking his chops.

"You have, um, lion blood all over you." A ridiculous sentence I never thought I'd say.

He grunted, gaze fastened on me with intimidating focus. To the point that I averted my eyes.

"And you do not like this?"

"N-not really." I tripped over my words.

He studied me with his eerie eyes some more. Long enough that I began to get antsy. He suddenly turned toward the water, striding forward and across the shallow end, his stomping sending water splashing at me. I flinched from the freezing liquid splattering across my bared skin. A low hiss accompanied steam with each inch the water touched his body. He waded in until he submerged himself fully.

I climbed to my feet. It was so cold, and this dress was doing nothing to protect me against the elements. Probably wasn't helping myself by being near the water. I backed up, rubbing my arms.

The spot where the lions attacked him was coated with blood, and he'd literally left nothing else. Hopefully that would hold him over so he didn't feed on my family. Water rippled as every part of him except his antlers went under.

"Are you ready to go back to the shack?" I called, shuffling from foot to foot. Would he hear me under there? He emerged, and I took some more steps back, wanting to be out of range when he shook his body.

"No." He approached on all fours, prowling toward me. Steam came off him like crazy.

"Can I go—" He pulled me toward him with a sweep of his arm. My legs dangled as he held me up and walked under the awning of a tree. He adjusted me against him as he settled on his side. I gasped and his arm tightened around my back, pressing my face to the damp fur on his torso. Honestly, I would have expected him to be much wetter than this.

"Why are we staying out here?"

"I want to." He grunted.

Even damp, his body felt so much like a furnace that I was sure he'd be dry soon.

"What if something attacks while we sleep?"

"Nothing can harm me." It wasn't a boast, it was a statement of fact. The surety made the hair lift on my arms. Fenrir was a true predator, and he held me in his claws, claiming that I belonged to him.

I struggled to stay awake, but his furnace-like body lulled me into giving in to exhaustion. I was so tired and he was a nice warm, toasty furnace. I cuddled in closer.

"If nothing can harm you, why were you so hurt when I found you?"

He stiffened, but my silence seemed to calm him. A low growl vibrated against my cheek.

"Humans took me as a youngling." The disgust coating his tone when he said humans almost hurt my feelings, but if they'd taken him like he said, I couldn't fault him. "They will regret capturing me."

The ominous statement sent a chill up my spine.

I wasn't sure if I'd be able to fall asleep with how on edge I felt, but it was awfully comfortable against him . . .

SUCH SWEET, delicious bliss awoke me. Lust licked up my spine, setting me aflame. Everything in my core clenched for something to hold onto.

The hardness pushing against my butt flared my desire more. I ground back, needing more pressure to get rid of this agony gnawing at my senses. A solid arm crossed my chest in a diagonal, and I hugged it to my chest, sinking my fingers into the silky fur. Awareness crept to the forefront, but my body felt too good. I squeezed my eyes tightly shut, riding the wave of lust.

Since my body felt weightless, I hugged Fenrir's arm like he could anchor me. A low whine vibrated in my ear and his gyration shoved his large cock against my back. Damp material clung to my spine and backside.

I didn't care because this felt so damn good. I moaned, grinding against the bulge. My clit pulsed, desperately needing relief. Sliding my hand downward, I delved under my dress, shoving my fingers against the throbbing pulse of my sex.

I gasped, jerking from the touch of my fingers. Fenrir's claws flexed and one of his sharp talons pierced the front of my dress. Fenrir's arm stiffened and then clenched me tighter to him. His cock twitched against my spine and the damp sensation intensified.

Suddenly, he flattened me onto my back and leaned over me, his muzzle hovering over my face. I panted, staring into his glowing eyes.

The heavy weight of his cock settled on my stomach and twitched. One of my hands was still between my legs so his wet shaft pressed against the length of my forearm. I ground my palm against my sex. Electricity spiraled through my limbs, wrenching a cry free.

His glowing eyes flared bright, then he tore my dress straight down the middle. Even the yank of my dress enflamed my desire. His eyes fell over my breasts and the glow flared. I looked down to see my brown nipples puckered.

His head cocked. I breathed so hard my chest moved up and down in a disjointed movement. Slowly, oh so slowly, he lowered, and his tongue lashed across the tip.

My spine arched off the grass.

"That feels so good," I half whimpered. His eyes flashed

brilliantly, even the strands of fur intertwined with his dark fur. Then he repeated the lick. His cock twitched against my bare belly, spilling a little bit of glowing cum across my skin.

He nibbled the tip of my breast and I moaned. My weak arms slid to my sides. It took everything in me not to grab onto his antlers.

"Yes," I breathed. "More. Please. Yes."

"I will claim you." He jerked my hips up and toward him. He was about to turn me onto my knees.

"Wait," I cried out, bunching the fur at his chest.

He snarled and his eyes drained of all light, leaving nothing more than a shadowed figure looming above me. I froze and struggled to breathe.

"Fenrir?" I whispered.

"Mine." His claws spanned my hip and he forced me down. The wet tip pressed against my core, even just the tip felt too wide to enter.

"W-wai—." He plunged forward. I screamed, my head falling back. Tears flooded my eyes, trickling from the corners.

A pleased grumble vibrated his chest.

"More. Take more." He snarled, thumping his claws into the compact ground next to my head. Agony flared at my sex. Burning agony. I whimpered from the pain, shifting to try to relieve some of the pressure.

"You have to wait." I panted, tears welling.

The orange glow returned to his eyes and he cocked his head, slightly drawing his head back.

"Why do you leak again?"

He leaned down and his warm tongue swiped across my cheeks and temples in an oddly soothing motion. While he cleaned my face, I worked to relax my tensed legs. He was so big, how was he even halfway inside me?

My pussy fluttered around his cock, and I exhaled slowly. His tongue slid across my collarbone. Oh, that felt really good. My shoulders relaxed from their position near my ears. He licked me again, coaxing a moan from my throat. Heat built in my core and my channel throbbed around him. That felt really good too. I gasped as lust speared through my gut. Desperation to move gripped my hips, so I did.

He groaned and the unrestrained, wild noise caused a throb through my core. He made me so wet. He curved his body, keeping himself sheathed inside me, and with a bow of his head, his tongue flicked down to graze my nipples again.

I moved my hips in a circle again, wanting more of him. His cock stretched me until the top of his shaft pressed against my clit. Fenrir grunted and thrust forward again. This time, there was no resistance and although there was a pinch, his cock and my sex were so wet that it made the glide seamless.

His tip nudged so deep it stole my breath, but he continued to push the rounded curve at the base of his cock inside me until he was fully seated inside me.

"I will rut you," he bared his teeth. Withdrawing his cock came with a sinful, wet sound. I could feel moisture leaking out of me with how turned on I was.

He slammed back in without allowing me a breath, I gasped.

"Yes, whimper for me, human." The dip of the thickness at his base popped out wetly. A whine crawled free. I did what he ordered, because I couldn't help it.

He slammed inside me again and again, taking, claiming, devouring and I rode an unfamiliar pleasure blooming between my legs. He'd made me orgasm before, but this felt like it came from a different place. More intense, more visceral. My fingers clawed into the grass and foliage, crumbling dried leaves. I felt tighter than a bowstring.

His next rut tossed me into oblivion. My hearing faded until I could only hear my violent heartbeat madly pumping in my ears. Whines spilled from my lips, mingling with pleas.

"Fenrir," I whimpered.

A vibrating purr echoing from his chest raised the sensitivity in my body.

I dug my heels into the ground, thrusting up to meet his demanding pumps. The orgasm washed through my limbs with a crash, but I wanted more. My pussy throbbed around him, clutching him tight. I gripped tufts of fur on his chest, yanking and tugging. The vibration in his chest ratcheted up another notch.

His cock slammed into me hard, and he ground into me without pulling out. His fur pressed against my inner thighs. So so soft. I whimpered, grinding down on him. I didn't think it could feel any better, but then the thickness at the base of his cock swelled.

I stopped breathing.

His animalistic snarl reached through my pleasure. It swelled and swelled . . .

Warm cum jutted inside me. He roared, tossing his head back so he was framed by the moon. Such a majestic sight. I followed him over with moans and whimpers, gyrating on his thick, wet shaft.

My toes curled. My limbs trembled . . . everything in my body flared to life and I could feel every inch of him inside me.

I'd thought it was impossible for him to fit, but he was

firmly planted inside me. The mind-bending throbs subsided with each panting breath. Until I lay under him, an absolute puddle of pleasure.

Grass rustled under my shoulders. My hips remained at an incline; his palms lifted from the ground to cup my hips. The slight prick of his claws caused me to tighten around him. A guttural groan escaped his maw. Breaths huffed from my lips in quick bursts. My goodness, that felt unreal, yet, so unbelievably impossible I couldn't have conjured it in any fantasy.

Finally, my breathing leveled out so I wasn't a panting mess, but the pressure at my sex remained intense. I relaxed in his grip, expecting for his cock to slide out of me, but nothing happened.

Oh-my—I was stuck!?

"Fenrir, why can't I move?" My voice shook.

"I have knotted you." His chest puffed out. Was he proud about this? Knotted? What did that even mean?

His head lowered and he sniffed my temple, releasing another round of rumbling purrs. In response, my core fluttered around him.

I squeaked at the overload of sensitivity. Now that the wave of immediate release had abated, reality settled in. The ground was hard and uncomfortable. And only where his fur touched me was I warm. A shiver crawled up my spine.

Fenrir reached under me and in a smooth motion, he turned until I settled on top of him, still secured on his cock.

My legs fell wide against his waist and my clit pressed against his fur.

I gawked down at my stomach, there was a roundedness to my belly bulging out. His cock seemed to have rearranged my insides to fit.

"How am I not dead?"

"My release," he grunted, claws flexing into my thighs.

"Um, what?"

"Rest on me," he grunted, palming the back of my head to force me down. The bend forward pulsed his cock and knot inside me, eliciting pleasurable tingles.

I ground down, whimpering.

So, his glowing cum had side effects . . . I had no thoughts or words.

NINE

FENRIR

Her soft, fleshy mouth parted with a puff of air and she straightened again. Humans wore fabrics on their bodies to cover their sensitive skin, and I'd shredded hers. What was left of it lay in tatters next to us.

The round flesh on her chest swayed. Such interestingly arousing flesh. Only the human women had this aspect to their body and they always covered them. Curving my head up, I swiped my tongue against the hard protrusion. Her sex squeezed my knot.

I bucked without control. Her head fell back, and she clenched my fur hard, using it to keep herself balanced. They seemed to be some sort of arousal inciting button.

"What do you call these," I licked the tip again. Her sex squeezed my knot every time I did it.

"Breasts." She panted.

"Our females do not have these."

Her fleshy mouth became thinner.

"Oh." She flexed around my cock and it responded, wringing a shudder from her. "How did your cum make this possible?" She spoke haltingly, as if she struggled to push the words free.

I should not answer the human, but some innate desire forced me to sate her curiosity.

"It makes humans stronger." The humans experimenting on me enjoyed talking. From them, I learned much of what they had been doing to my species. There were other creatures they would take just for their release. They were milked for their cum to experiment on, to taste, to *discover*—they said.

The frigid slab I had been strapped to had been isolated from the other creatures, so all the information I had garnered was from the human's conversing. All I ever bore witness to was humans and how they enjoyed shredding apart my innards. Decades under their experiments offered me an insight on much. Especially how vile they were.

"Fenrir?" Her voice echoed in my ears, muffled by the ringing. I flicked them to shake off the remembered agony of being shredded open. "Hey, are you okay?"

Her voice was low and hurried. I focused my attention on her. Her mouth pursed and she cocked her head to the side.

"Okay?" What did she mean by this? She wanted an affirmative?

"Like are you feeling well?"

I wasn't sure what this meant. So I only grunted. I struggled to hold her gaze, so I gave up to peruse her oddly erotic body.

I ran my claw across a jagged scratch on her leg.

"What did this," I couldn't keep the fury from my tone. "Who marred you?"

The fur over her eyes lifted high.

"Um, you."

"I have not—"

"Yes, you did." Her fleshy mouth thinned again. "I came running to warn you and you said all sorts of things and then tossed me on the ground."

The image she painted was not as she said. She had charged me, her eyes wide and her teeth bared.

"You aimed to attack me."

"No, I was trying to warn you that the lions were behind you."

"Warn me?" I did not understand. "Why?"

Her body moved with her scoff.

"They were going to attack you."

I stiffened as if she had dug her little human claws into my chest. I could not form any words to come from my muzzle. I could not make sense of any of this. Nor the warmth in my gut that bloomed through my limbs, urging me to keep her at my side for eternity.

Her eyes did not glow, but they reflected mine. She stared at her little claws buried in my fur, moving them in scratching circles.

She had been petting me and I did not care.

Lycans did not mate how I took her. Facing each other— only through the male mounting. . . but I did not care. I enjoyed this little writhing human and the sounds she expelled.

I craved it *and her*. The small creature called to my instincts. She remained locked on my knot, claimed by me. A vibration rumbled through my chest. Yes, she would remain mine.

Her head pressed against my sternum. She nuzzled her cheek into me.

"Has anyone ever told you you're really untrusting, Fenrir?" Her sleep coated words seared me internally unlike I'd ever experienced.

The humans had given me that name, and I told her of it as a reminder of what humans were capable of. But from her human *mouth*, it now caused pleasure.

They'd taken me as an adolescent, stolen me. Tortured me to the point that all I knew was pain. My old life with kin remained in the far recesses of my mind. Before consciousness and awareness spawned with the Rift, I lived violently in my world. As a youngling I was allowed to stay with my creators— the ones to birth me, but I would have been expected to leave once I found my breeding match, except I'd lived trapped.

I'd bided my time, waiting for my strength to grow in order to escape. There was a reason humans hardly ever attempted to capture full grown monsters. They would have been shredded to pieces and devoured. Just as I'd done to many of the human males that hunted me. If I had been full-grown, they would not have been able to take me, but I took pleasure in knowing that even at my youngling age, I'd slaughtered two of them and maimed many.

Mia hummed and nuzzled my chest again. The warmth inside me throbbed like a live thing.

This little human was not the same. Lycans did not entangle themselves this way or touch the way the human touched me. I could not ignore her presence. It beat against my fur. Not unpleasantly. The opposite. I thrust up, jostling her on my knot. Her fleshy mouth opened with the sweetest sound, and her sex squeezed my cock.

I would keep her with me. Never again would I harm this gentle human, so unlike others.

Once I fed on the flesh of those vile humans who tortured me, I would not leave her side.

TEN
MIA

THE SWAYING MOTION OF BEING CARRIED ROUSED ME from the deepest, most comfortable sleep I'd ever experienced. I groaned, rubbing my cheek into Fenrir's chest fur. A low vibration echoed from under my ear and pleasant shivers crested down my spine.

"Where are we going?" I croaked, blinking the bleariness from my eyes. Each sway of his walk rubbed his thick cock inside me. How was he still stiff? His rough palms rested under my thighs, holding me perfectly against him. He was so large that his arms formed a comfortable nook. "You like to ignore me, don't you," I mumbled.

Fenrir grunted. Another beat of silence and he huffed. "Where I can leave you unexposed."

My eyebrows winged up. He actually answered. I didn't know if I was hallucinating, or there wasn't as much of the growly edge to his tone . . . and he hadn't made any mention about my hands on him. I clenched a bunch of his fur in my fist. He held me securely, but I still held on. A nerve felt pinched in the crevice where my thigh bent. My core felt raw, stretched and sensitive. I squirmed.

"How long will we be stuck together?"

The long line of his body went taut and he slowed his determined stride.

"You want to be rid of my knot?" He responded sharply, glowing eyes narrowing.

"It's just a question." I scowled.

He bristled at everything. Like he expected the worst at every turn. "You're super sensitive." He grunted again, probably not understanding a lick of what I said.

A familiar worn path caught the corner of my eye. We were headed back to the shack. If I could turn to look over my shoulder, I bet I would see it.

He moved past the tree trunks at an alarming rate. Perks of his massive strides. His arm tightened across my spine more securely and he bent forward, his chest getting all in my face and blocking my view completely.

Wood creaked and then I heard the hollow echo of claws scratching wooden boards. He tilted me while I clung to him. I sputtered, spitting some of his fur from my mouth. His hunched position straightened as much as he could inside the shack.

Fenrir dropped to his knees with a loud thump. Pinpricks tickled my legs. If I didn't move them, they'd become numb to the point of falling off. Even with him on his knees, if that was what that body part was called on his body, my feet didn't touch the floor.

The pressure at the entrance of my sex loosened. I gasped at the release of his knot. Liquid gushed down my thighs, making me feel like I peed. I stiffened, looking up at him. His glowing eyes settled on mine. Using his fur as a purchase, I lifted myself up, using my tingling feet to push off his hips. Liquid continued trickling from my pussy in a rush. Orange glowing cum painted the insides of my thighs.

"Oh," I breathed.

"I must clean you." He grabbed my hips, lifting me so easily, and laying me on the ground with care. I gawked up at him. His antlers stretched high over his head. Intimidatingly. He dropped to all fours, leaning over my sensitive sex.

His muzzle dipped and he began licking me clean with long, toe curling swipes. I twitched and jerked with every run of his tongue. I was much too sensitive for this.

"Fenrir," I yelped.

He grunted again.

I scowled at him. His antlers hovered a few inches above me. With the moonlight coming into the shack, I got a better glance at them. There seemed to be the smallest fibers coating the bone. Would they be soft if I touched them? He licked again, making my leg twitch.

"You taste . . ." He trailed off and I stiffened, battling with the urge to hide from him. All this was so new and scary. Even if I did like it.

"Like what?" I breathed, pushing myself to my elbows. "Bad?" I rolled my lips between my teeth and tried to close my legs. His rough palms flattened on my legs, splaying me wide.

"Unlike anything I ever encountered. I will never tire of it."

"Oh." I breathed, gawking down at his large head hovering over my wet, aching core. Orange flared so brightly it reflected on the walls and forced me to shield my gaze.

I laughed nervously. "Never is quite a long time." He didn't respond. His head moved with each drag of his tongue. The silky texture flicked against the inside crevice of my thigh, and I snorted out a laugh, trying to shy away, but his grip didn't allow me to.

"Fenrir," I gasped. "It tickles."

"Tic-les?" His tongue flicked out in the same spot.

"Tickles. It feels funny." I explained with a guffaw.

"You do not like this? Then why is the fleshy mouth covering your fangs spread like when you moan with pleasure?"

Fleshy mouth? What the . . . "Oh, my lips?" I pointed at mine. "You're asking why I'm smiling."

"Smiling." He nodded, his ears flicking. The inside was as pink as his perpetually wet cock which had sunk back into his slit at some point.

"What are these named?" His sharp claw raked up the swell of my belly and rasped against my nipple. His head tilted questioningly.

"Nipples." Another drag and the sharp talon was much too close to my face.

"Muzzle."

"Nose and mouth," I corrected. He seemed so confused, it was cute.

"You are very different from a female lycan." He'd already said that. I scowled.

"Um, yeah, makes sense since we're different species." My tone held the slightest bite, but his words rubbed me wrong. I tried to jerk my leg away, but it was no use. His finger-pad grazed against something that stung, and I hissed a breath out between my teeth.

His nose flared and he dipped, sniffing. I tensed. What on earth was he doing? He forcefully moved my left leg so it crossed my other thigh. His glowing eyes flared, but since he wasn't looking at me, I saw what held his focus. His nose neared the long scratch on the outside of my thigh. Little droplets of blood gathered along the wound.

"You are leaking red now." His snarl echoed off the walls of the shack. He must have grazed his claws against the scratches and re-opened them.

"It's just a little cut." I scowled down at the wound.

"I will heal you."

His palm flattened behind my neck, and he forced me up, bringing me to my knees while he rose to his with ease.

A loud huff blew my hair back as he lowered his muzzle to sniff me and his cock emerged from the slit.

"What are you doing?" His grip on the back of my neck flexed. "How can you still be hard?" I gasped.

"You."

He pulled me toward him so fast I put my hands on the sides of his thighs before I smacked face first into his bobbing cock.

"Be still," he ordered, pulling me closer.

"Fenrir." I shoved at his large, oddly jointed arm.

"I will heal my female." Heal my female? . . . Heal with his *cum*? He'd been healing me. The realization smacked me across the face. The scratches really had been as bad as I'd thought. They'd started to heal from the first moment he forced my mouth to his tip.

He looked down at me from high up, taking hold of my chin between two claws. If I moved my head, they'd rip through my cheek.

"Fine," I huffed.

He was already moving before I said anything. The single-minded monster would not be swayed. Fenrir did as he pleased.

"Taste me." Both my eyebrows went up on my forehead. The order reached into my gut and roused desire to life.

"Fe—" I choked on my sentence. The rounded tip of his wet cock shoved against my lips and stopped my words. He rammed his hips up, forcing past my lips. My jaw creaked with how wide I had to open my mouth.

Tears flooded my eyes, and I tried to speak, but was unsuccessful.

I sank my teeth into the tip before he rammed right through my esophagus and killed me via cock impalement. That would be so traumatizing. He hesitated at the feel of my teeth, and he jerked back, giving me the chance to turn away.

"You have to be gentle." I gasped. His head cocked. "Do you want to kill me?"

He recoiled, his large grip releasing me. His cock bobbed in front of my nose. An orange glow reflected off the pink, wet shaft. The base had already started swelling. Cum beaded at the tip, the orange color making my mouth water. I could taste the remnants of his sweet precum on my lips and I licked it clean.

"I do not want your death," he rumbled in his growly voice. The corner of my lips helplessly twitched up. He sounded so scolded. Like how I sounded the time I accidentally over-watered the roses wrapped around the front of the house, causing them to wilt and die off.

I gripped the base, right above the knot. The knot pressed against the side of my pinky and palm. That massive base had swelled so much inside me—and I'd taken it—and loved it.

I wet my lips and leaned forward, pressing against the head

where his moisture leaked. The sweetness exploded on my tongue. It tasted so good I couldn't hold back my groan. I peeked up at him. He was laser focused on me, his upper lip curled, exposing his deadly, sharp incisors.

Gliding my palm up, I squeezed hard. A loud rumble vibrated his body. I flicked my tongue out, licking the flat of it around the protruding tip. There was the slightest ridge circling the head.

When I moved my hand down, a guttural groan exploded through the room. I did it again, rubbing up his shaft and licking the tip, swallowing the sweetness he offered me. Warmth flowed through my veins. My eyelids lowered. So delicious. I stretched my mouth around him, working to fit my lips around the head. A flick of my tongue caused his hips to twitch, driving his cock further in.

His tip shoved against the back of my throat, making it difficult to breathe or swallow. I pointedly grunted and he relaxed his thrust.

The stretch to fit him wasn't as painful, but I could still only fit about three inches of him inside my mouth. I eased off him, licking as I lifted.

A draft kicked up and movement caught my attention. He was wagging his tail. I peeked up at him and his eyes were closed, head tipped back.

How . . . cute.

Lust bloomed in my gut and expanded outward. Dipping my head, I flicked my tongue up the shaft. Cum dribbled down the sides and I lapped it up, taking all he offered.

A needy whine escaped the terrifying monster. Having him fall apart because of me made me feel powerful. I wet my lips. His pleasure made me want to slide myself on him again, but I wanted to see him come undone just from my mouth. Taking him with both hands, I gripped him, my fingertips struggling to touch with how large he was.

One squeeze of his length caused a gush of release to spurt into my mouth and I swallowed the delectable taste. I wrapped my lips around his tip again and pumped his shaft, stopping at his knot.

His hips twitched with each of my movements, but keeping hold of him kept him from ramming into my throat and breaking my neck.

A whine spilled from his muzzle and his claws tangled in my hair, gripping it hard. The pinch faded with the gush of release from his cock. I shivered, pumping and licking, relishing in every inch of the monster's cock.

Heat traveled down my throat and spilled through my veins, chasing away the slight chill of the early morning. He shuddered, head falling forward, his large body bending.

"Why didn't you swell as much?" I ran my fingers over the dip of his knot.

He let out a very canine groan and swept me in his arms, swiftly tucking me under his body. His body vibrated with a rumbling purr.

He was really soft and the rub of his fur against my skin comforted me. Since he rested the majority of his weight on his side, with me nestled against him, and slightly under him, he enveloped me.

I rolled to face him and cuddled closer.

A smidge of guilt speared my chest. I shouldn't enjoy fucking a monster this much.

"You will remain here until my return."

"Where are you going?" I stiffened against him.

"I will return." That didn't answer my question. Would he go feed on Jason and Pam? Panic squeezed my lungs.

"Fenrir," I hesitated. His head cocked, glow falling over my face. "While you're gone, I will go—" His growl cut me off. The hair on the back of my neck stood.

I PRESSED MY PALMS INTO HIS CHEST AND A RUMBLE vibrated under them.

"You will not leave." There was no threat in his tone, just simple statement of fact. I blinked, flabbergasted, and tried to wrap my head around his demand. He hadn't even let me finish my sentence.

I sank my fingers into his fur again. He seemed to melt into my touch when I ran my fingers through the thick warmth. Unlike before, every time I touched him, he seemed to savor it. "Fenrir," I started, drawing out the end of his name.

His orange glow flared, as it did whenever he seemed to experience a strong emotion. Ever since he'd washed off and fed, blood no longer spilled from his injuries. He seemed strong and he'd stopped walking gingerly.

"Human. You will do as I say."

I rolled my lips inside my mouth. I'd sorely underestimated his lack of humanity, which was incredibly illogical on my end considering he was monster. Maybe 'humanity' wasn't the word I was looking for. I'd underestimated his lack of compromise.

"You're being unreasonable." I clenched his fur in a stiff grip, tugging hard, but he didn't seem bothered by it. I glared up at him. Frankly, I was the unreasonable one by expecting a monster to listen to what I said. A strong, large monster that could end me with a flick of his wrist.

Shoving my palms against his chest, I managed to wriggle to my front, but his grip hadn't let up so I gave up and lay with my cheek smushed against the floor boards. I struggled to catch my breath. He was so heavy!

"You're hurting me," I mumbled, muffled and miffed. His grip immediately loosened, allowing me to climb to my knees, and I sat back on my butt.

As soon as he left, I would take off to warn Jason and Pam to hide. Then be back in time for him not to know I'd left. That would solve all my problems. Or I could leave with Pam and Jason. My stomach dropped at the thought. I scowled up at him. What had he done to me that the thought of never seeing this creature again messed with my head? He smoothly climbed to all fours.

"Listen. While you handle what you have to—"

"You will stay." His head swung in my direction, his pointed furred ears flicking side to side.

I opened my mouth then closed it. With a clearing of my throat, I said, "Yes." He was too stubborn to reason with so I would have to lie. He could think I stayed and for all intents and purposes, all he would know was that I *did* stay, as long as I covered my trail. He seemed to have an extra strong nose.

He chuffed loud enough that he fluttered the hair framing my face. Now that the smell of blood no longer coated him, the underlying scent I'd smelled on his fur had become prominent. Pine and fresh air. I laced my hands on my lap, studying them, hoping with every fiber of my being that he couldn't tell I was lying.

"A human once said he would release me," he started, inching forward, oh so slowly. I stiffened as his muzzle hovered over my forehead. "He did not."

"I will stay put—"

"Silence," his voice boomed. I sucked in a breath, my heart pounding so hard it thumped in my ears. "Your sweet scent . . ." He sneezed. "Your scent is off." He snapped his teeth in my face. Breathing became more difficult. I'd frozen in fear. "Enough."

I clawed to the string of sanity pulsing through my scrambled brain.

"Y-you're scaring me."

He drew back as if offended.

"Fear, I smell it." He sneered. "I will not harm you."

"Hard to believe with you snapping your teeth at me." My voice trembled.

He huffed so hard my hair fluttered around my bare shoulders. I hugged my chest, suddenly feeling how naked I was.

"You are mine. I will not hurt what is mine." He said it with such finality. As if his claim was a statement of fact. I narrowed my eyes up at him.

"You already have," I retorted, wanting to see what he would say back.

Fenrir loomed over me, a growl ripping through the shack. His large grip wrapped around my bicep, and he pulled me to my feet with ease. I stumbled after him. He seemed dead set on dragging me to the corner of the shack. He gently urged me against the wall.

"What are you doing—no!" I shouted.

Fenrir bent one of the rusted old pipes over my waist, securing it around my hip and stabbing the other side into the wood. It burst through the wall and he shoved again, lashing it around my waist. The rusted bar dug into my belly, effectively trapping me. I wrapped my hands around the metal, shoving and pulling in panic.

"Wh-what is this?" I choked out. "Fenrir, what are you doing?!"

"I will return." He studied me and as if coming to a decision, turned to the swaying door.

"Wait." I uselessly yanked at the flaking metal. "How long will you be gone?"

He shoved the door open, his fur fluttering with the draft from outside. Without his body as protection, the chill seeped into my veins.

"If you're leaving me here, you owe it to me to give me *some* answers!"

"I will not be gone long." The glow in his eyes intensified. Pam used to talk to me about heaven and hell and Fenrir seemed like a creature straight out of those biblical tales. A shiver coasted up my spine.

"Fenrir!" I struggled against the harsh edges of the metal bar. "Fenrir, don't leave me," I cried. He stiffened and loped back to me. The glow from his eyes fell across mine and he pressed the sharp tip of his claw under my jaw.

"I will be back for you." His tongue slid across my cheek, catching half my lips.

"Wait," I cried, panting. If he walked away and came across Jason and Pam; he'd kill them, I had no doubt. I couldn't let that happen.

"Leave Jason and Pam alone." Maybe I could wiggle down

and get out of this makeshift contraption once he was gone. I froze in place before I could clue him off to it. "Please, don't hurt them." Emotion throbbed through my gut. "I swear I'll do as you say and stay put, but please, please, leave my family alone."

"Your?" His muzzle curled. "Nothing is yours. You are mine. Belong to me. Only me."

He loomed close to my face. I made sure to stay still, holding my breath as he snarled in my face.

"I will kill any that take your attention from me." His head cocked.

I clenched my eyes closed from the onslaught of his glow. I leaned against the wall, letting it support my weight. When I opened my eyes, he was gone.

The window allowed a faint yellow hue to reflect inside. The sun was just beginning to rise but it would be hours before the day warmed up and I'd turn into a popsicle if I didn't get to warmth, especially since I was naked.

I gripped the cold bar digging into my stomach. It wasn't so tight that it restricted my breathing, so if I sucked it in a bit and slid down then I could get out of this. Only problem was my boobs and head.

I wiggled down an inch and the rust caused the bar to abrasively rub against my skin. Copper flakes fluttered to the ground.

Once I reached right below my breasts, I flattened my shoulders against the wall. Bracing my hands on the bar, I used the wood at my back and the strength in my thighs to push with all my might. Just a little more so my breasts could fit. Strain burned through my muscles. I could do this. After all, I was the one to carry things around here, I could do this. I gritted my teeth and gave a final heave. The bar groaned in protest, but it moved enough. I inched my hands over my nipples, squeezed my eyes closed, and yanked down. Scrapes abraded my skin across the side of my boob and all my knuckles. Now just my head. Wrapping my hands around the bar, I braced again, managing to get a better grip at this angle. I pushed with gritted teeth, and it moved a few more inches with a squeak. I panted, dropping my clammy hands. Turning my head, I inched down. Pressure became excruciating near my ear, but I gritted my teeth, pushing through. I bit back a whimper and finally extricated myself.

At least I was finally free.

I popped to my feet. Fenrir seemed like a single-minded creature set on killing the people that had taken him, but if he caught the scent of my parents . . .

I pounded down the steps and onto the forest floor. Leaves, pebbles, and branches crunched underfoot. I winced at the assault on the bottom of my feet, but continued forward, hugging my breasts so their bouncing didn't hurt as much while I ran. In the last decade I'd lived here, I'd never ran through the woods nude. It was not a comfortable feeling.

I wove around a protruding branch. The chickens in the coop went crazy as I passed them.

Jason's wide brimmed hat moved within sight. I crested over the slight hill and the rest of him came into view.

"Jason," I shouted in relief. He was okay—he was alive. He popped up to his feet. His eyebrows rose high on his forehead as his gaze dragged down my body. The small shovel in his hand thumped on the ground next to the flowers he tended. He yanked the gloves from his hands and tossed them to the side as we approached each other.

His blond eyebrows furrowed, meeting in the middle. A quick scan was all he needed to do. His gaze lingered on the swell of my breasts peeking over my arms wrapped around them.

My face burned with embarrassment. He took hold of my shoulders, looking down at me with a stiff expression.

"What have you been up to?"

"A monster took me. He was injured in the shack—"

"You're naked," he cut off the start of my babbling, not seeming to process what I was saying. Or if he was, he was too focused on scanning my body. My face burned hotter. I dropped my eyes to his chin, embarrassed about what I'd done with the monster. For enjoying it so much, and even worse, for wanting more.

"I-I . . ." Anxiety swelled my throat, making it difficult to push out an explanation.

"Why are you fucking naked?"

I'd never heard him sound like this, it was usually Pam that cursed up a storm. Jason was always quiet, reserved, watchful.

I didn't understand the anger marring his features. The hot flush spread down his neck and a vein popped at his forehead.

"Answer me, what have you been doing?" he said lowly. The hair raised on my arms, my instincts bidding me to pull free from his hold and run. I shook my head. This was Jason. He'd raised me, he wouldn't hurt me. I struggled to swallow.

"T-there was a situation." I grappled for words. Not knowing what I should say. All I wanted was for them to hide, or leave, just until the coast was clear. Jason's fingers dug into my arm. The slight stabs of his nails weren't as painful as Fenrir's claws, but it still smarted.

"You're hurting me," I croaked. His grip barely loosened.

"Is that a hickey?" His eyes narrowed on the swell of my breast. What was a hickey? I followed his gaze to the red spot on my boob. On the top side there were the slightest marks. I knew it had been either the graze of Fenrir's fangs or the scrape from escaping the pole, but it looked like a nibble of teeth from this angle. He scoffed, grip becoming hard again.

"Stop making shit up. What have you been doing?"

I blinked.

"I . . ." I shook my head hard, eyes wide. What was he saying?

He pulled me after him, dragging me into the house and up the staircase. I tripped, but he didn't stop to let me gather my footing. The side of my leg scraped unpleasantly against the carpeted step.

"I ordered you to stay away from the other side of the lake." He shouted. "A boy found you over there didn't he?" I trembled so hard. "Didn't he!?" Tears dripped off my chin. I couldn't make sense of what was happening.

"Pam," I shouted, half sobbing.

"Quiet, girl," he hissed.

"Why?" I shouted, fighting fruitlessly. He kicked open my door, dragging me toward my bathroom without answering my question.

Vomit crawled up my throat. He shoved me into the bathroom.

"Wash yourself clean of his filthy touch."

"Mia?" Pam called from downstairs, a question in her voice. Jason's eyes narrowed.

"Pam," I shouted. He slapped me hard enough to rattle my teeth. My legs gave out and I fell to my knees. I clasped my face, my eyes wide on his. What-I-This didn't make sense. My face crumpled.

"I will take you to see her once you shower," he said. "Stand up, Mia." I struggled to get my legs under me. He shoved me forward once I was up and I stepped into the large bathtub.

"I-is—"

"Yes. The pump and boiler are on." That wasn't what I was going to ask, but mentioning Pam right now was a bad idea so I clamped my lips shut. He'd lost his patience . . . and his mind.

I turned the handle and water spouted from the shower head. Cold water spit at me and I shivered, hugging myself. He pulled the glass door shut, preventing the water from escaping but still letting him see me. Once the water warmed, I grabbed the rag I used to scrub my body and rubbed the homemade bar of soap on the fabric.

He watched me, eyes hard. I swallowed and scrubbed my body almost violently, as if I could scratch away the crawling sensation of him watching me.

"Do not get out until I return for you." His eyes seemed like they belonged to someone else. They were maddened—as if he'd snapped. My stomach soured.

He slammed the door shut. The lock snicked from the other side, trapping me in the bathroom. A long time ago, he'd installed the doorknob backwards . . . had it been on purpose this entire time?

TWELVE

MIA

I HELD ONTO HIS PROMISE OF TAKING ME TO PAM AND bathed the sex and dirt off me. I scrubbed at the little marks on my body. Most of the scratches had been healed up thanks to Fenrir's cum, but the mark on my chest had happened in the scuffle of trying to free myself.

The water was beginning to cool, so it had to have been a while since he left. I eyed the bar the towel hung on. I could use it as a weapon . . . the doorknob clicked and twisted. I quickly shut the water off. My fingertips had become prunes. Grabbing the towel, I swiped it across my hair quickly and wrapped it around myself. I carefully stepped on the towel laying on the floor.

He approached with a slip hanging over his arm.

"Put this on." He grunted. "I like how it hugs your curves."

I wore this dress often during the summer, from the day that I turned fourteen when he'd gotten it for me during a run to trade for materials. I'd been so happy about wearing it, especially when he complimented me, but I'd thought it had been innocent. A father to a daughter type of compliment. I dropped the towel and it pooled around my feet. I'd struggled to escape the wrong monster.

My hands shook as I tugged on the dress he handed me. The thin buttery fabric fell against my skin. All I wanted to do was tear it off. It'd been irreversibly tainted.

To make matters worse, I was so cold my nipples poked through. I hugged myself to avoid his hungry gaze.

How had I been blind to his lust? Had he felt this way for me since they found me? Nausea churned in my stomach. His gaze dropped to my feet and he backed out of the bathroom.

Poor Pam. Had she known? I would ask her as soon as he brought me to her. His evasive comments about her didn't settle well in my stomach. Jason re-entered and crouched to place my slippers on the ground.

His head hovered low, attention downcast. I could grab the soap container and bash it across the top off his head. My fingers curled, but before I could lunge, he straightened.

His eyes, hovering just a few inches above mine, settled on me with satisfaction.

"Perfect. Now come make me dinner." His gentle prod against my shoulder went against everything that had been happening. I curbed my urge to flinch away from his touch.

"What about Pam," I choked out. He paused and flicked his eyes to the side, his mustache wiggling.

His palm settled on my shoulder, squeezing once as he guided me down the steps. At the bottom of the banister, he urged me in the opposite direction of the kitchen. Down the thin hallway to their bedroom. The door was ajar and with every step closer, my stomach twisted until it couldn't get any tighter.

Jason nudged the door open with the tip of his shoe, urging

me forward. I stumbled, catching myself on the bed. The mattress dipped under my curled fingers. The bottom of Pam's nightgown draped along her shins. I slowly followed the cloth up to her face. She lay with a serene expression and her hair a wild mess against her pillow. She looked asleep, but something was off . . . she wasn't breathing.

"Pam," I breathed.

Pam lay still. Frighteningly so. I pressed my hand into my stomach. Please, please, move . . . I had heard her call for me.

I slowly approached and nudged her shoulder. Her arm flopped off her stomach and onto the mattress with a heavy thud. Her chest wasn't moving.

"There, my girl. Now we don't have anyone between us."

I remained frozen, unable to move. To breathe.

His hands wrapped around my biceps and he nudged me away from the bed. We had nothing between us . . . had he planned this all along?

Pam didn't deserve that. He must have suffocated her while I showered. A broken sob ripped from my throat. Why was this happening? I didn't understand any of this.

"Shut it," he shouted. I clasped my palm over my mouth, muffling my cries. "Now make me some breakfast, my girl," he said. He always called me that, but it had never sounded this disgusting.

I snapped myself out of the thick numbness creeping over my thoughts. If I gave in, I would become a puppet. I needed to keep my thoughts clear to escape him. He guided me to the kitchen. A few feet away was the same stove Pam taught me to cook on. Hours upon hours of her going over instructions.

"Why did you kill her?" I croaked.

His eyebrows furrowed, a deep indent appearing on his forehead. The familiar face had turned into one of a devil.

I'd thought Fenrir was a monster, but I preferred him to whatever evil stood before me.

"Mia," he murmured, palm cupping my jaw. I stiffened. Revulsion keeping me stiff. "We don't need her anymore. Now that you're a woman, we can be together," he cooed.

"Have you been waiting for me this entire time?" My lips felt numb every time I talked. Like I floated outside my body.

"No, no, dear, I'm not a perverse man." He said it with such assurance. He believed what he was saying with his whole body. "But a man can only control himself to a point." His thumb caressed my cheek. "There comes a time where he must satisfy his urges." A load of words that meant nothing.

I struggled to swallow.

"Did Pam know?" I tried so hard to keep my voice from shaking. Maybe I could escape if he thought I wanted this too.

Jason sighed, his mustache twitching with the movement of his lips.

"She started to suspect, but only a night ago she walked in on me touching myself in your bedroom." He sighed again. "We've been waiting for you to return."

I stopped breathing. "Here I thought you were spending your time working, not being a whore." His words turned into a hiss.

"I wasn't," I croaked. A lie and I couldn't hide the reddening of my face. His eyes turned into slits.

"You belong to me."

He leaned down, his familiar face coming much too close. His lips fell on mine and vomit rose in my throat. No. I could not do this.

I drove my balled fist into his stomach. He doubled over and I whirled to make my escape. He lashed out and grabbed my wrist.

I didn't want this. Please, let this be some horrific nightmare. My heart felt like it was about to explode. I dug my fingernails into my palm as I tried to pull my wrist out of his grip. Wake up. Wake up! He yanked me by my forearm, forcing me to face him again.

His nose touched mine, the look in his eyes searing into my soul.

I wasn't sleeping. And there was no escape.

Fenrir would have stopped him . . . if he hadn't left me.

I paced through the woodlands. They must die. Every single one of them, especially the *scientist* that enjoyed carving his way into my chest.

I lifted my nose, tracking my scent back the way I had come. There had been no rain, so it should be strong enough for me to follow. Travel would take time, but if I did not stop, I could return soon. What she had had of my release would hold her over until my return.

Vengeance would be mine . . . but my human.

I slowed to a trot, rounding a tree again.

Leaving her behind . . . I did not want to and it caused me to pause and pace since I left her. She eventually stopped screaming for me, but I couldn't force myself past the boundary of the property. Destroying them would not take me long. I would return once I avenged myself. Another few paces forward and I slowed again. The distance between us grew and I did not like it. I slashed my claws through a trunk.

The human had ruined me.

I could not leave her.

A far-off scream, familiar and fearful caused my ears to twitch. That was my human. Mine! A roar burst from my chest, and I sprang forward.

This was not the screaming anger I had left her in. This was pained and frightened.

No one was allowed to frighten my female.

FOURTEEN

MIA

Right before his lips fully settled on mine, I turned my head to the side, letting out another shrill scream as loudly as I could.

"Don't touch me," I said, choked, tears blinding me. I couldn't act. And even if I could act like I enjoyed his touch, vomiting all over him would have given me away.

This wasn't Jason. The one who'd taught me how to set traps, how to live. The one who'd raised me. Sure, sometimes he seemed annoyed with Pam, but-but—

His fingers dug into my arm. His nostrils flared, gaze thinning. He yanked me after him with ease even though I fought him. My slipper fell off in the scuffle.

I let myself go limp and managed to get out of his hold. I lunged for the pan on the stove, simultaneously swinging.

He caught my wrist, stopping the iron before it thwacked him across the temple.

We struggled with the pan and I used every ounce of strength I owned to yank, but it was no use. Rage contorted his features, and he hit my wrist so hard that the pan thudded on the linoleum. His palm slammed into my chest, right between my breasts. My spine hit the dinner table. I yelped. He came at me in the same breath, grabbing my wrists and stretching them over my head. My spine bowed as his weight fell over me, my feet barely touching the ground.

"Stop, please, Jason. Stop," I sobbed. He stiffened over me, breathing hard. Everything stilled. His hips remained nestled between my forcefully spread legs.

I shivered, bile encroaching.

His touch made my skin crawl, and I wanted to sink into myself. I felt dirty and gross.

If Fenrir hadn't left . . .

Tears pricked my eyes. The monster wasn't so bad, he'd been gentle recently and every time he'd hurt me had been unintentional.

"You need to learn a lesson, Mia."

I understood where this headed now that I'd been with Fenrir, and it made me physically sick.

I'd rather die than be forced by him. He yanked my arm to the side so he could hold both my wrists with one hand. The one he'd unoccupied slipped downward. His fingertips grazed my nipple.

"Please, Jason." I whispered. "No." But he didn't stop.

He gripped my breast, and fortunately the dress served as a barrier.

"Such a beauty." He squeezed much too hard. Tears spilled from the corner of my eyes. "Do you know how many times I've wanted to lay you on this table?"

He was sick. Finally, he let go of my breast, and reached down to yank at the zipper of his jeans.

"If you want to behave like a whore. I'll treat you like one."

I screamed, bucking, but he flushed his hips against my sex to pin me down. The hard bulge was nothing like Fenrir's.

Tears silently flowed down my face as he used his hand to free himself.

I screamed again. This was it—

The door ruptured open and a snarling monster burst through. My monster.

"Fenrir," I cried. Everything after that happened much too fast. My monster moved with frightening speed, so much so that Jason hadn't had time to let go of my wrists before antlers were speared into his body, poking out from different parts. Blood gushed and splashed across the room, catching me as it sprayed. He wheezed and then stilled, going limp above me. The only sound was Fenrir's heavy breathing. Jason hung off the antlers. They protruded from his gut, chest, arm, and out of his eye socket. The plink of blood dripping onto the linoleum echoed to my ears. I lay frozen, with blood sliding down my cheek.

Fenrir backed his oversized body up, taking my adoptive father along for the ride as I slid limply off the edge of the table onto the floor. I shouldn't even call him that anymore. He never cared for me like he should have cared for a child. Not if he had been able to do what he'd done to me . . . what he planned to do to me. I followed Fenrir's movements with my eyes.

He lowered his head and lifted his claws. He was about to swipe *him* from where he was impaled.

"Wait!" He froze. "Can you do that outside?" I struggled to push words out of my throat. There was already enough blood I would have to clean.

He only grunted and his long fluffy tail swished as he left through the broken front door.

He'd snapped the wood straight in half. Hopefully I could fix it, because if there was no door, then it would get too cold in here and . . . I squeezed my lips into a line and shut my eyes.

I curled on my side. Something to take care of another day. Pam's still form flashed behind my eyelids. Everything had changed from one day to the next. My family was dead . . . I was alone. Utterly alone.

A wet touch on my cheek urged my eyes open.

Fenrir pressed his nose into my forehead and then a long tongue flicked across my cheek. I crawled to my knees and threw my arms around his wide, large neck, clinging to him. I fisted tufts of his fur, holding on like I could disappear into him.

His arms hesitantly snaked around my waist, flattening me to his chest. Hard enough for me to feel secure, but not fearful that he would pop me like a balloon.

His nostrils flared.

"Your scent . . ." he said gutturally. "You don't need to fear any longer."

He exhaled so hard it blew my hair backwards. I clutched onto him tighter, and a rumbling purr vibrated his torso. Soothing me. I no longer feared Fenrir. A human's face, one I trusted with everything inside me, had been the true monster. At least Fenrir seemed to want to care for me. His version consisted of a lot of licking, but I couldn't complain too much considering what I'd faced with Jason.

I started to slide downward, and I tightened my grip in his fur, clawing my way back up with my heels digging into his sides. His claws pricked my spine, tightening me to him— squeezing me to him. I rested my cheek against his fur.

Sharp teeth grazed against my shoulder. The rasp of them didn't break skin. Goose bumps exploded down my arms. His pine scent flared my need more. I needed to be touched and held. To erase Jason's touch.

"I need you," I said, muffled against his fur. His purring stuttered, grip tightening painfully. "Fenrir?"

He'd become immobile.

Vulnerability coated my words, but I wasn't sure he would be able to distinguish the emotion. By his stiff reaction, I doubted it. I ran my palm against his side, rubbing my fingernails into his fur. He jolted as if electrified back to life.

"I will do as you say," he said gruffly.

Those were words he had not uttered. Until now, it'd been whatever he wanted and that was that. A fresh wave of emotion swelled in my chest. A mix of exhilaration, relief, and something that felt an awful lot like affection.

"Get me away from here," I mumbled, poking a finger in the direction of the stairs. I kept hold as he followed my guidance. The stairs groaned in complaint under our weight, but they held, sturdy and strong. The hall was wide, but still his large body rubbed against both sides, and he had to lean forward to avoid his antlers scratching up the ceiling.

"That's my room." I craned my neck. He bowed low enough that I would have been dangling from his neck if he didn't hold my lower body against him. I wiggled until he set me down.

He settled on all fours, slowly inching his way around the room, sniffing. He rumbled with pleasure. "Your scent coats your den."

He peered at my drawers, lifting an elongated hand and poking it with a long sharp talon. A rasp of his nail later and then there was a long line in the wood.

"You have to be gentle." I pursed my lips and hurried to his side to grab his arm. Fenrir kept turning his head side to side as he scanned every inch of the room. Even if I couldn't read expressions on his face, his confusion was clear. I bunched his fur. He turned his large head toward me. I tugged him until he began following me to the bed.

"Lay down," I murmured. Fenrir stiffened.

"I will not be bound," a crisp anger filled his tone. And the slightest panic. I took a step back. The people he'd been hell bent on killing had irreparably hurt him. Based off his reaction, something I'd said reminded him of it.

"I will never, ever bind you, Fenrir," I whispered. "Or hurt you."

The stiffness melted away from his body as he watched me and he finally lowered.

He was able to lay flat on his back. Although my bed was big, his legs still dangled from the edge. My lips twitched.

"I'm going to get on you. Is that okay?" I inched forward, hesitating.

He only grunted.

I climbed up on top of him, straddling his waist. As I scooted upward, I felt the hard bulge in his slit. Inching higher, I braced my palms against his chest, and leaned forward until I could press my lips to the side of his long muzzle.

He chuffed.

Something hard poked into my back. A rumble vibrated against my hands. I hadn't felt him harden and emerge.

"I'm going to ride you, Fenrir." His glowing eyes flared brightly, illuminating my bedroom and casting the bright light against my breasts. Using my thigh muscles, I lifted up to scoot back until his thick cock pulsed in front of me.

Taking hold of his wide girth, I poised him at my entrance. He shuddered at my touch.

The wet pink cock twitched. I lifted higher and the hem of my blood splattered slip dress pooled at my waist with how wide I had to open my legs. Holding him still, I inched down on his tip.

I wiggled my hips, working my core down until I enveloped the mushroomed tip of his cock. So big. I hissed, my clit throbbing. I was so needy my channel pulsed around the tip of his cock. I rocked my hips back and forth, taking another inch of the bulge. It was my turn to shudder.

A peek up at Fenrir showed him watching me steadily, his chest rising and falling harshly.

"You are . . . delicious."

Fire licked up my spine. His hips twitched, driving him into me a bit more. I whimpered, my eyes lowering halfway. He felt so good.

"Take more of me," he growled. My body responded, relaxing to glide down even more. I couldn't breathe. I could feel him deep in my throat. There was still much more of him I hadn't fit inside me, but this angle made everything feel intensified. I panted, wiggling.

I widened my thighs and relaxed with a breath. That did away with the resistance, and I settled fully on him, my sex rubbing against his fur. His knot pulsed and expanded. My head fell back on a moan.

Fenrir bucked his hips up, thrusting into me and jolting me on top of him with ease. Forcing me to ride him. The steady thrusts verged on desperate. Moans spilled from my lips. I ground down with twists of my hips, feeling every inch of him take me.

My channel clasped his cock and in a sudden explosion, I orgasmed. It came upon me in such a rush that I screamed. He thrust up and forced me to take the base of his swelled cock. His fur rubbed against my sensitive clit and I whimpered.

A whine left his muzzle and my channel gripped him tighter, another orgasm chasing the last.

I forced my eyes open. I wanted to see him lose control. His teeth were on display, a snarl marring the monster's features. He stiffened, hips lifting me high, forcing the knot deep. I fell forward, curling my fingers into his fur. His sex throbbed inside me. Each jolt of release caused me to spasm on top of him. He jostled me on him as he thrashed beneath me.

Fenrir filled me up—claimed me. But now, I *wanted* to be his. To remain safe in his violent arms.

Panting, both his and mine, filled my bedroom. I slumped forward, settling on his chest, deliciously stuck us together. I nuzzled his wide chest. My forehead rested on the part that would be his sternum on a male human, but considering he was much much larger, and a monster, I didn't even know if he had a similar bone structure. Not that it mattered, I was all in with him.

I petted his fur, running my hands through the thick strands. We lay on my bed and my mind wandered as I relaxed into him. He'd come back for me. He'd saved me from Jason forcing himself on me. I rubbed my cheek against his silky fur.

If he hadn't come for me . . . I licked my lips. Not something to haunt my thoughts since it hadn't happened.

He suddenly stiffened.

"I have hurt you." What was he talking about? Fenrir took hold of my hips and pulled me off his knot. I yelped from the sudden give of my sex. The pop of release washed liquid down my thighs. He put me on my back.

He sniffed in again. In a smooth glide he inched downward and gripped my thighs to keep me in place. His wet nose pressed into my pussy. I jumped from the shock.

"Blood."

I hoisted myself onto my palms to peek between my legs. Mingled with his cum were hints of blood.

I didn't feel hurt, but . . . I mentally counted days and realized I was menstruating. He was talking about my period blood. Heat flushed across my cheeks.

"It's normal." I laughed nervously, flushing.

"Normal?" He growled, alarmed.

"When I'm not pregnant—"

"Breeding?" His eyes flared bright and he exhaled hard.

"Y-yeah, breeding. Like after—" I started again, hesitantly. Stopping when he snarled.

"I will fill you with my seed. I will breed you and you will no longer bleed." He announced firmly, like it was a done deal.

I floundered for words, slowly backing up. I'd already inched to the edge of the bed. I looked at the door, then at him. He seemed wild . . . animalistic. I wasn't exactly scared of him, but breeding me? No thanks.

I licked my lips.

"Um, I'm going to go get some water."

"Do. Not. Move," he snarled. He bared sharp, sharp teeth. "I command it."

His eyes flared so brightly it blinded me, but in the same breath, the color leaked out and they became devoid of any glow.

The hair on the back of my neck stood on end.

I threw my body off the bed, using every bit of momentum I could to get to the door.

FIFTEEN
FENRIR

I SLAMMED HER TO THE GROUND, AND SHE FELL TO her knees with a cry. It was enough to satisfy my urge to hurt her for running from me. She belonged to me. Me. Only me.

In one lunge, I had her face down in her den. Her scent surrounded me, causing my cock to remain stiff, aching, wanting.

She yelped, her hands clawing into the floor in front of her.

My human would not escape me. I curled my paw under her stomach, forcing her hips up, offering her glistening, wet sex to me.

"Fenrir," her voice lowered. Her voice spiked through my cock, filling it with the nectar of my release. I would offer it all to her.

I lowered, pressing my nose into her succulent offering. I ran my tongue across her sex. Her blood coated my tongue. Even though it tasted different from the liquid that spilled from her eyes, it was just as savory. Every morsel of her invited me in —trapped me.

With my second lick, her small body relaxed, and a whine left her lips. My hips bucked forward in answer.

Maddening human.

I licked her again and again, stealing the nectar from her core. I shoved my long tongue into the tight depths that gave way to my ownership.

My hips bucked again. Need thrummed and I could no longer ignore it. Positioning her before me, with my claws pressed into her sides, I presented her to myself. She remained supple and giving to my lead. Her sex throbbed, begging for my dominion. Liquid dripped down her slit. I pressed the tip of my cock against the soft flesh. She twitched her hips and I could no longer contain the rutting urges. I rammed into her sheath. She would be filled with my seed until her belly expanded from it. I would breed her and fill her with my young.

A shudder worked over my spine, my fur standing from the agonizing pleasure. I could not control myself. I rutted desperately, slamming her on my aching knot. Forcing it inside her.

Small whines and whimpers left her lips. The rhythmic sounds of my breeding her swelled my knot with painful pleasure. With every graze of her soft sex shoving onto my knot, I strained. Her channel clasped around me, squeezing me in its straining sheath. The human was small, but my release allowed her to take my girth. To savor it. If she had not had it, my claim would have killed her.

She trembled, screaming as her sex squeezed around me. I did not stop.

I would fill her. She belonged to me.

Only me.

She screamed again, bucking against my cock like a female in breeding heat.

Yesss.

She would never leave me. My little human would always belong to me.

I curved forward, keeping my violent pace while overwhelming her body. Such a tiny thing under me. My human.

My female.

In a lunge, I sank my teeth into her shoulder, digging my canines deep into her flesh. In the same move, I slammed her hard onto my knot. Her blood exploded on my tongue. Unlike any taste. Unlike any human I had devoured.

She screamed again and she bucked against me desperately, her sex squeezing around me. I whimpered against her shoulder. Her panting caused my knot to expand, locking me inside her.

Release came on at the end of my knot locking her to me. Every one of my limbs trembled. Bliss spiraled down my spine and I roared.

My cock spilled with wringing agony.

I had claimed the human as mine and no other would do. I caught her as she fell forward, holding her to my chest as I leaned against her nest. The soft fabric gave way to my weight. She had odd human items in her den. Ones I had never seen. I nestled her to my chest so she could be comfortable. Hard surfaces were no issue to me. They were what I had grown used to.

The walls of her sex squeezed me. I shuddered, huffing in pained pleasure. I nestled her spine against my front, running my claw against the fur on her head as she usually did to me.

"Fenrir." She stopped speaking. I held still. What would she say? If she wanted to escape me, it would not happen— "Do the females of your species bleed?"

It took a moment to understand her question.

"Yes, when they are ready to breed."

"Well, it's a little different as a human. We bleed after we're 'ready to breed' as you put it. So the way it works is whatever isn't used . . ." The lull of her voice soothed me. She continued speaking, but all I could focus on was how her sex clasped my cock.

Yes, little human, whatever you said.

I held her to me as she continued speaking. My knot incrementally softened, and she moved. Would she try to leave? She twisted and her frail, weak hands sank into my fur.

Instead of showing fear or running away, she climbed on me, clutching me tight.

A shiver coasted up my spine and a low rumble vibrated my chest. My body jerked and I found myself leaning into her touch. She yanked her hand back.

"Sorry, I forgot you're not into touching."

I carefully lifted her wrist and set her hand back where it had been.

"You are different." The comment rumbled from my throat. Her large eyes blinked up at me and her small features became red.

I cocked my head to the side. What did this mean? Humans were expressive and I was coming to learn that there was a reason behind every reaction her body offered.

Her blunt claws scratched my neck, running upwards in a sweeping motion until she reached my ears. The rumble in my chest made her petting pause.

"Are . . . you . . . purring?"

"I do not know what 'purring' means," I said. All that mattered was that she continue scratching my fur. I forced her hand back against my chest, forcefully rubbing it against me as she had been doing.

"You are mine, Mia." She must know her truth. There would be none to take her from me. To touch her as that disgusting male had attempted.

"Yours?" Her eyes widened up at me.

His claim repeated in my head. Fenrir had said that to me before, but this time it felt different. What the hell was going on . . . and why did I like it? Unlike when Jason said it, Fenrir's announcement curled pleasure through my chest.

My stomach continued to somersault.

I finally felt safe—because of him. The swell of memories rushed forward. Jason had attacked me. He'd kissed me and touched me. If Fenrir had not come for me, he would have taken me like . . .

I burst into tears.

The monster I clutched onto stiffened.

"Have I hurt you?" He growled. His voice turned gruff and almost unsure. Something that was clear about him was his difficulty with inflection. Most of the time, there was none, other than anger. His chest rumbled with a sound different from when I pet him. It was one of anxiety.

His tongue lapped across my cheek, taking the tears with it, but they were soon replaced.

"My human." He rumbled between the licks to my face.

If I wasn't wrong, it seemed like he was trying to comfort me?

"Don't leave me like that again." My next sob came with such force that it wracked my body. His arms wrapped around me like a cocoon. In a smooth glide, he rose and sat on my creaky bed, gathering me on his lap. He easily settled me against his warmth, enveloping me. My temple settled near his sternum and his large arms corralled my sides. Such a large monster . . . I sighed and leaned all my weight against him.

"I will not leave." He chuffed. He rubbed his palm down the side of my head. The large double joined appendage pretty much wrapped around my whole head. "You are mine." He repeated his earlier words. The declaration was as much a promise as a threat. But it comforted me. I was alone in this world now. All I had was Pam and Jason and they were both gone.

Fenrir, a monster, had saved me from Jason's assault, the man that I thought of as my father. Another sob ripped from my throat. Fenrir's growl shook my body.

"Where are you in pain?" He snarled. I sniffled, trying to get it together. I was freaking the monster out.

"I'm just extra emotional," I choked out.

"Emotional?"

Sigh. How did I explain so he could understand?

"Sometimes, I have big feelings, and I need to let them out. Don't get too worked up about it, I'll be okay." His tongue flicked out, catching strands of the hair framing my face. He did it again and again. He was cleaning blood and tears off me.

"I can just go shower," I croaked after a moment. A bit hesitant because it felt good—relaxing.

He ignored me as he liked to do, and his tongue lapped

against my temple. He smelled good, like the forest. Even with all that blood on him.

So much of Jason's blood.

My stomach twisted with discomfort.

His cock roused and emerged from its slit. The thickness pressing up into my side. He groaned and he pressed the front of his mouth to my neck, nibbling. I snorted and jerked within the cage of his arms.

"You're tickling me," I said between guffaws. Tears stopped forming on the heels of his attack.

A rumble vibrated in his chest. He pulled me nice and tight against his large body, flushing me against the length of his front.

The wet glide of his shaft prodded against me insistently. I shuddered, eyeing the bead of precum on the tip.

I touched the glowing liquid and popped my finger in my mouth. My eyes slid shut and I hummed, swirling my tongue around my fingertip to collect it all.

"Feed from me."

His demand curled under my skin, making me want it. The vibration seemed to reach into my stomach.

I wanted more of his licks. It'd felt good being at his mercy. It was incredibly wrong for me to crave this, forbidden even, but I didn't care. I wanted the beast and his harsh ways. I wanted those vibrating rumbles enveloping me as he pumped deep inside, then locked me to him.

I hungered for the safety and comfort he offered.

His shaft twitched, expelling more need. He seemed ravenous for all of me.

His claws gently flexed into my arm. I groaned. I felt sticky and bloody. A shower called to me. One to wash away the dirty memory of Jason.

"Not right now," I slapped his paw off my hips. It did nothing to get him to release me, but at least he stopped to look at me.

"Fenrir, no."

"You do not want me?" He said it low, and the words were so guttural it was difficult to make the sentence out.

"You are so dramatic," I huffed. He tilted his head.

I pressed a kiss into his furry muzzle.

EMOTIONS WAS WHAT SHE CALLED THE LIQUID pouring from her eyes. Such an inconsequential, non-threatening liquid, yet it caused some odd shifting in my chest. It urged me to destroy everything that dared make her leak it.

If I had not shredded that human male already, I would have done it over and over, and much slower. I learned much of torture at the hands of humans.

"I'm going to shower."

I stiffened my grip on her.

"You will not leave my sight."

The fur over her eyes scrunched close together.

"You're coming with me," she announced, lifting only one of the fur strips above her eye.

I grunted in answer.

Anything she pleased, I would do. Even to 'shower'. I lifted her, taking care with my sharp claws and placed her on her feet to the side of her nest. She wobbled and I kept hold of her until she slipped out of my grip.

Sliding off the nest and dropping to all fours, I followed on her heels. Much too close. My claw caught her leg and she gasped, stumbling forward. I swiped out to catch her before she slammed onto the floor.

"Did I harm you?" I asked, alarmed with her silence. Turning her, I took hold of her leg and lifted. No injury. I had not hurt her. I relaxed. She flailed her arms around as she hopped on one leg.

"I'm fine! Put my foot down," she shouted, her arms waving in the air. "Down, Fenrir." My ears twitched at the volume she emitted. I slowly lowered her limb, and she huffed. Seemingly . . . upset?

"What have I done?"

She eyed me. Looked down and then up at me.

"Nothing," she said, and lifted her palm to rub the side of my neck. Her small face was angled up toward me. Her hypnotic eyes studied me. I could no longer have much distance between us. If she traveled with me, I would keep her safe and hide her nearby the compound I'd been held in. It would only be moments that I would be gone. Kill the humans and then collect her and return to this den. We would make this place ours. I would breed her with my young and she would never leave my side. If she continued to feed from my seed, she would live as long as I did.

"You will come with me." She stopped petting me and her *lips* turned downward. I was beginning to take note. When she did not like something, they made that same movement.

"Wait, what?"

"I am not leaving you." I already informed her of this. Why was she shocked?

"Hold on, hold on. This came out of left field." She put up her hands. "Where are we going?"

"The compound."

She blinked.

"You mean the place where they hurt you?" Her voice lowered. When she spoke this way . . . I fought the urge to pace. I grunted in answer.

"Not yet." She put up her hands.

I exhaled hard, a growl building in my chest.

"No, no. It doesn't mean I won't go at all, but first I need to shower." She shoved her little claws through the fur on her head. "A-and I need to fix up the house and clean all the blood and—" I licked her mouth. She became silent.

Waiting a bit more will not change my course.

"Very well."

She closed and opened her eyes quickly.

"Very well? What does that mean?"

"I will do as you say."

Her body stiffened and she seemed not to be breathing. What was wrong with her? The corners of her lips kept twitching.

A pleasant tinkling sound escaped my human. Her mouth was stretched wide. "Are you sure you're a monster?"

"I am a monster," I responded. I believed that was clear. The pleasing sound came from her again.

No human had ever made such a sound. This was like a lycan's vibrations. Indication of pleasure. My cock hardened, emerging from its slit.

I would destroy any creature to hear her vibrations again.

"Let's go shower?" she asked, voice still breathless.

I waited for her to guide me to whatever this "shower" was. She walked straight, toward the hole across from her nest.

I took care not to hurt her legs as I followed. She turned into a compartment smaller than the one filled with her scent. She stopped in front of a small box and reached inside. Water began to spurt from a nozzle.

What was this? I approached slowly, needing to be on all fours as I entered. My sides rubbed against human things.

She lifted a foot and walked into the small box. She pulled a pane that would close her inside. It would trap her!

"Mia," I snarled, lunging for her arm.

She screamed and hugged her arms to her chest, staring at me with wide eyes. She looked side to side, showing too much of the whites of her eyes. Prey tended to peel their eyes this way when they feared for their lives.

My claws were wrapped around her small limb and I loosened my grip.

"What happened? What is it?" she breathed, calming her panting.

I eyed the white box, lifting my lip in a threat.

"This will trap you."

Her mouth pinched together, then she burst into that tinkling noise. The fur on my body lifted.

"This is a showerhead." She pointed at the thing spitting water. "I fill the water up and it comes through here heated instead of all cold like the lake." She inched under the falling water. Her head-fur plastered to her skin. "Come in." She waved her hand toward the empty space that dipped into the box.

She stood in it without a care. I did not trust it. Returning my attention toward her, I studied her wide eyes. She would not harm me. She *had not* harmed me. I grunted and followed her, carefully climbing inside. My tail hit against the box and it rattled.

"Be careful, the glass will break." She clicked her tongue as she arranged the barrier back in place.

My head hovered over the bar holding the *glass* up and I could see outside of the smooth hole we stood in.

"This is a showerhead—" Water sprayed across my muzzle, blinding me. I sneezed, turning my face away from the assault.

"What is this attack," I snarled. She would not harm me, but the water continued to pelt me. I sneered at this 'showerhead'.

She aimed it down.

"It's not an attack," she mumbled.

"I want none of this." I set my front limb on the edge of the bowl to climb out.

"Wait," she cried out, bunching my fur in her little fist. "You need to shower," she said, her chin tilted upward. "Fenrir, please." Her lips turned downward. She was dissatisfied. I did not want her dissatisfied.

I gritted my teeth and sat on my haunches. The fit was tight and uncomfortable because the pane pressed against one side and my other side was flush to a white wall. "I'll not get your face this time. Promise." She angled the showerhead she held in hand toward my neck. Rivulets of water traveled down my fur, weighing it down. I studied her human face. Her dark fur, the gentle curve of her small muzzle—no, lips and nose. There was nothing that should call me to claim her. Nothing about her resembled a lycan female. Yet, I only wanted to mate her. Her sex still smelled of desire and blood. Her body ached to be filled with my seed so she could breed.

My cock stiffened and expanded from my slit.

"Whoa there, Fenrir, let's get through a shower." The corner of her lips lifted. That expression right there, that was what I liked. And especially when that tinkling noise escaped her mouth.

I could watch her move for eternity. Focus settled over my instincts, narrowing in on this female.

I no longer had the urge to run. Once I devoured those that harmed me, I would be content to lay with her. Just this little human in front of me.

She rubbed a bar of some floral-smelling thing on my body. "What is this?"

"A bar of soap. I made it." Her mouth tipped up, and an airy sensation expanded in my gut. My cock throbbed to life.

"What is that?" I lifted my claw to the corner of her lips where they went downward. "Do not make them go down," I snarled. The showerhead spit water on the ground as she held it lower.

Her eyes widened.

"You don't want me to frown." *Frown*. She frowned again, and I sneered. That was what she was doing? There were so many parts to their human language. And this one was not the only language. After devouring a human, monsters absorbed the language of the one they fed on, so I understood the humans but not always the meaning behind the words.

"You're so cute," she said with a smile. "Lean down."

I dropped my head as she ordered. She slid the bar around my horning and ears. Water dripped into my eyes, stinging. I growled and yanked back on instinct.

"Wait. Fenrir, wait!"

I shook my fur out. She sputtered, lifting a hand to block

the spray erupting from my fur. I settled, the sting no longer present.

She swiped her face with the back of her hand, taking away the white foam that left my fur and attached to her.

My human did not seem pleased, but her huff only caused a swell in my chest.

EIGHTEEN
MIA

I EYED THE POSITIONING OF THE WOOD. I'D NEEDED to fix the broken slab with some extra strength wood glue. Fortunately, Jason had been a hoarder, so I'd found everything I needed in the shack behind the house.

Fenrir held the door up for me to make sure it was lined up perfectly. He'd been my little assistant. Quietly studying my movements with such focus that he bore holes into my face.

"A little more toward you," I said. He did as I asked, dropping it a bit. The hinges lined up with the door frame perfectly. I slipped the screws in and took the screwdriver in hand, turning the handle as fast as I could, forcing the bolt into the hole.

I looked up at him. His eyes flared bright, and I squinted.

"Dampen the glow," I winced.

He grunted and did as I asked. His ears twitched, flicking side to side. The tips of his antlers almost touched the ceiling when he fully straightened. Good thing the ceiling was so tall. Unlike in the shack.

For a monster, he was incredibly patient with me. But he was taking his statement about never leaving my side to a dramatic level. He literally didn't leave my side. No, he refused to. That was a more accurate description. He'd developed a clinging fixation.

Since he'd proclaimed that he would take me with him, he hadn't said anything to me about leaving. But I could tell he was growing increasingly antsy. He had one thing left to do and he was fixated.

I'd exhausted myself by cleaning up and making sure the crops were making progress. Now, the clean-up of the house was about to be done.

Returning to the place he'd been tortured shadowed my every thought too. It would be time very soon. I couldn't keep holding off. But I kept wanting to. What if they managed to capture him again. Or kill him? My stomach soured. I finished turning the screw until it could turn no more.

I tossed the screwdriver into the tool bag. As I stood, I brushed my hands on my shorts.

"Where are you going?"

"To feed the chickens," I said. The front steps creaked and the gravel crunched under my weight. My thigh muscles burned as I climbed up the incline toward the coop. Chickens squawked and flapped with a flurry. Fearfully.

I peeked over my shoulder. Fenrir loomed up right behind me on his two back legs.

Feathers littered the front of the enclosure. Some feathers even clung to the metal chain link fence as if there had been a violent struggle. Was that blood?

I abruptly stopped and whirled on the monster.

"I told you not to eat them." I scowled at Fenrir. He grunted and lowered to all fours.

"They are delicious little snacks . . ." He trailed off, staring toward the coop. I shoved his arm.

"Fenrir," I snapped.

"Fine. Fine." He growled.

"You need to go while I get them settled."

He stared at me, not moving. I crossed my arms and lifted an eyebrow.

A harried sounding huff left his muzzle.

"Fenrir!" I threw my hands in the air. He was driving me crazy. He drew up back onto his back legs, looking down at me. Even with him watching me like that, with violence brewing in his posture, I didn't fear him. I scowled up at him and crossed my arms.

"I will leave you be." The announcement almost sounded angry. With that, he took off, disappearing through the brush.

I thinned my lips, watching the brush sway with his retreat. My shoulders dropped more and more with each second I didn't see him.

My stomach twisted. I took a step forward, about to chase after him. An orange glow flared within the forest.

He watched me. I sighed with relief. He hadn't left me. I could still feel his gaze even though I couldn't see him.

Getting the space I'd wanted made me feel yucky. I rubbed my arms and hurried to the coop. A tube of homemade feed sat next to the gate. I grabbed the scooper and carefully unhooked the metal latch to slip inside. The faster I worked meant I could go find Fenrir sooner. As much as I griped about him following me, I'd grown used to his presence, so I made quick work of spreading the feed.

He was all that took up my mind. No longer did I hunger, or even use the bathroom, all I craved was him. It was so weird, but it had everything to do with his monster cum. He'd explained a bit of what he knew about it after I'd pried it out of him.

I navigated around the seventeen—now, fifteen chickens and exited the gate. I set the scooper on top of the feed as I scanned the area.

Leaves crunched and I followed the sound.

"Fenrir?" I called, walking deeper onto the pathway. The dirt was disturbed past the shack. Claw marks marred the ground. "Fenrir. Stop avoiding me."

I came upon him as he reached his long arm inside the ground and dirt flew, raining down behind him. I stopped across from him, at the edge of the hole and crouched. It was shaped like a small human. A fine layer of dust covered his face, but he didn't stop.

"Why are you digging a hole?" I licked my lips nervously. Had he changed his mind? Would he kill me and—

"For the dead," he said, clawing deeper into the ground.

The air vacuumed out of my lungs. Dirt kicked out behind him. He seemed so concentrated on digging. I took one step back, then another. My nose burned with the building emotion wanting to burst free. I swallowed with difficulty.

He stopped suddenly and cocked his head to the side. In a smooth glide, he loped across the ledge of the hole.

Panic squeezed my throat, suffocating me. I backed up so fast my heel caught on something.

"Why do you smell of fear?" He snapped, moving toward me. I put my hands up.

"J-just make it quick," I croaked and squeezed my eyes

tightly shut. I couldn't believe he'd already gotten tired of me. Tears pushed behind my eyelids.

Seconds passed where nothing happened. The panicked shroud that stalled my thoughts slowly lifted. He exhaled hard and blew my hair back. If he wanted to devour me, he wouldn't leave anything behind *to* bury. I peeked out of one eye. He studied me from only an arm's distance away.

"What are you doing?"

I blinked quickly. Even though doubt had already crept forward, I had to hear it from him.

"Are you going to kill me?" I whispered.

He recoiled like I'd smacked him.

"Why would I kill you?"

"You're digging a hole in the ground . . . for the dead." I was so confused. He chuffed and he'd never sounded more annoyed.

"This is for your . . . family." His voice dipped slightly as if unsure about the word.

"My . . ." Pam.

I'd mentioned the human custom of burying humans after he said they did nothing for their dead.

This was for Pam?

Tears prickled my eyes. I'd been avoiding entering her bedroom, but a smell was starting to seep under the crack of the door. I didn't have it in me to enter.

"You believe I would kill you?" He rumbled. "You are my female. I protect mine."

I scrubbed my face with my palms.

He turned around, his large form retreating. His tail swished behind him. He didn't stop at the hole to continue what he was doing but continued past it.

"Where are you going?" He didn't stop at my question. "Fenrir!"

"Leaving. My female does not trust me."

Wait, what? Panic squeezed my chest.

"Don't leave. Wait!"

He ignored me. I chased after him, but his stride was too wide for me to keep up with him. My heart pounded in my chest like the wings of a hummingbird and running after him wasn't helping my pulse. He was right, I hadn't fully trusted him, but it stemmed from fear. I'd lost everything already, and I didn't want to lose him too. I pushed myself to run faster, even as I lost sight of him in the brush.

"Please, Fenrir," I cried. I didn't realize how much I cared for the monster. He was much kinder than I thought a monster could be, and I struggled to trust it.

"Do not panic, little human, I am right here."

I whirled to face him. He stared at me from a few feet away. As if he'd been standing there the entire time. I hadn't even heard him approach.

"Don't do that." I ran up to him and threw my arms around his waist. His vibrating purr reached through my body and squeezed my heart.

"I will not leave you."

I squeezed my eyes shut, rubbing my cheek against his soft fur.

"Never?" My voice trembled.

His palm pressed me closer to him.

"You will never be rid of me." I sniffled and hugged him as tight as I could. A perk about a monster? I could hug him as hard as I wanted.

He swept me into his arms, lifting me to his chest. I nestled against him, trusting that the limb he settled under my butt would hold me up.

"Thank you for taking care of Pam's body."

Fenrir's chest vibrated in answer.

I CLAWED MY FINGERS INTO HIS FUR, TRYING TO HAUL myself up his large body aaaaaand slid back down to my feet.

"This is pointless." I threw my hands up in the air. "Just go without me." His head swung to the side so fast he almost gouged my eye out with the sharp tip of his antler. It shouldn't be this hard to grab onto him since he was on all fours.

"I will not leave you behind."

"Are you sure?" I shuffled from foot to foot. I looked back at my house. Nerves squeezed my stomach. "I'll just hold you back."

"Up. Now," he growled.

"Jeez, okay, I'm going." I gripped tufts of his fur and hopped on my toes to get momentum.

He lowered closer to the ground, practically laying down. That helped me get a leg up. Fenrir jolted up, angling to the side to have me fall in place. The ground was way too far down. I leaned forward, scrunching his fur in both hands to keep hold of him. Close call with him being too large for me to spread my thighs around him, but fortunately, I managed where his waist tapered in.

"This is scary," I said, voice shaking.

"I will not let you fall." His voice vibrated through his entire body.

I was counting on it. I squeezed my legs tighter as he began walking forward. His strides so long they ate up the ground. What would take me six steps to cover took him one.

"And you're sure you'll know how to get back?" I looked back at the house as it became smaller and smaller in the distance and soon disappeared. Having never left the farm before, I would be as lost as a fawn. His pace jostled me to the side, and I scrambled to hold on tighter to the bunches of his fur in my hands.

"Yes."

He was beginning to sound exasperated. The intonation was low, but very present. A new tone unlocked. Something dramatically different than the toneless, growling voice he'd had when I'd found him half-dead in my shack.

As a monster, he may be instinct driven, but he was capable of learning and understanding.

"Okay," I mumbled and squeezed my arms tight around him.

"When your weak human body grows tired, say so."

A YAWN STRETCHED MY MOUTH, and I wiggled my toes within my shoes. My legs were numb to the point of aching. I'd succumbed to the lulling sway of his body and fallen asleep at some point. Surprisingly, I'd stayed mounted on him, but it was at the risk of having my legs fall off from the position.

I flexed my cramped fingers into his fur to stretch out the appendages. I sat up on his back, my body aching, and rubbed my eyes. Everywhere I looked was forest stretching further and further. The thick brush inclined to our left. I squinted, looking into the dense forest line. It seemed so dark within the crush of foliage. Fog coated the ground closer to the top, lending to an ominous and frankly, scary view.

"What's that way?" I squeezed his fur with one hand and pointed up at the dark shroud with my other.

"The Rift."

I stiffened. Pam told me a lot about the Rift. That was where monsters came from. Where the earth had split after the San Andreas fault line ruptured from the catastrophic earthquake and spawned their world into ours. Crossing the Rift meant death according to her. I shivered and hunkered lower against Fenrir. I trusted him to keep me safe.

"Are we going to cross it?"

"No." Fenrir's ears twitched and his body tensed under me.

I relaxed my stiff fingers. I hoped we arrived soon. My legs were starting to pulsate from all the moving I was doing.

"So how much longer—"

The rattling of chains cut me off. Leaves and branches crunched, and a large green forearm burst through the compact foliage to our left about ten of Fenrir's strides ahead. He slowed. He'd been aware of someone approaching. Another one burst through, followed by large, tall bodies. I huddled closer to Fenrir.

"What are they," I whispered.

"Orcs," Fenrir's voice rumbled, no intention of staying quiet. Like a collective, they all turned their heads. All five of them. So big and . . . they carried weapons strapped to their person.

Fenrir growled, lowering his head, displaying his antlers.

One of the smaller Orcs put up her hands. By her slighter stature, breasts, long hair, and narrowed features, it was clear she was the only female Orc. The four big ones behind her took their weapons in hand like they'd choreographed it.

"We do not want problems, Lycan."

The actions of those four behind her said otherwise. Fenrir only snarled.

"Fenrir," I whispered. My stomach hurt. One of the males to her side met my eyes. The vibrant shade of his yellow eyes glowed.

"Do not look at her." Fenrir shook so much that I struggled to keep hold of him. He felt like he would burst.

"We will pass without waring with you. Ignore us," the female said. A chain rattled, drawing my attention to one of the Orcs and the chain he held that was connected to a woman's wrists. She was without shoes and tears streamed down her face, silent but prevalent.

I gasped and my fingers flexed.

"They have a human," I breathed, starting to slide down.

"Stay," he ordered. I stopped moving. "I will not war." Aggression bled from Fenrir despite his words. The female Orc inclined her head at him while the others sneered, following her lead as they moved along, heading up the mountain, toward the Rift.

"But Fenrir—"

"No." His snarl shook my body. "I will not risk you. I do not doubt I can destroy them. But you will be left vulnerable. There are too many of them, one can take you—"

He went quiet, a violent growl melding into his words. "You are the only one I protect."

Fenrir and I watched the Orcs trek up the incline. The girl trailed behind, listless. Her chains rattled with each of her steps. My lip trembled. She seemed so sad and the clothes she wore seemed so dirty and tattered.

Tears flooded my eyes. This was the life I'd been ignorant to. I understood it existed, but seeing it was different. I'd been so sheltered up in my little piece of the world. Even before Pam took me in, I didn't remember anything other than sleeping on the ground and that was as hard as I'd had it.

I'd truly been lucky until Jason went crazy.

Fenrir lifted to his back paws. The sudden shift jolted me and I began to slide down his back. I would have fallen if his arm hadn't propped me up before bringing me to his chest.

"Do not leak, human. I will not allow anything to harm you."

I burrowed my face in his chest, breathing in his pine scent.

"It's called crying. Not leaking." I sniffled.

It was a good thing I'd never been allowed to leave home. I would have been eaten alive.

Not everyone could be saved. I understood that, but it really sucked—that poor girl—I needed to get my mind distracted.

"So . . . what you are . . . is a lycan?" Pam and *him* never referred to the creatures as anything other than 'monsters.'

"It is what humans have named my species." He released a snorting huff. "You humans enjoy placing things in boxes."

"So those Orcs were also named by humans?"

"Yes, before the Rift, we would not have consciousness to name ourselves."

"You almost sound sarcastic," I mumbled.

He grunted, continuing on the path in silence. I squeezed his fur, holding onto him tight.

I swayed within Fenrir's arms. He'd been carrying me for a while now, fortunately, because my legs would have fallen off if I was still on his back.

Rocks crunched under Fenrir's weight. Trees had dwindled until a concrete jungle replaced the forest we'd just been in. He entered a cement pathway lined with large buildings that almost blended with the night sky. I'd never seen structures that were so tall. I gawked up at them, awed by the climbing vines clinging to buildings. The forest seemed to be sucking the concrete into its embrace. Rubble littered the sides of streets in all shapes and sizes. This felt like a completely different world. I sneezed from the heavy scent of smoke.

I squinted at little bits of stuff floating in the air. Putting my hand out, I caught some on my palm. Ash.

"I think something is burning."

There was more than I ever thought out in the world—everything that I'd known about but never experienced. And never wanted to experience again. I'd been blessed living in a bubble. I valued my home more than ever now. Jason would leave to collect things we needed. More so in the earlier years. The trips had tapered off gradually as he stored as much as possible.

"We are near," Fenrir said.

I tightened my arms around his neck. "Something is not right." His nose wiggled as he sniffed.

He sharply turned and ducked through an alcove. A stone ledge was nestled to the side of the building. Hidden by the destruction. His arms hoisted me high on his chest and he propped my butt on the ledge.

"Do not move until I return." He rubbed the side of my head like he was petting me. I scrambled to grab ahold of his arm.

"You're going to leave me here?" I gasped, eyeing the steep drop. I peeked behind me. It was a little nook. A pretty deep one from the look of it.

"I will return."

"Fenrir." He leaned to lick my cheek.

"Calm, my human." He watched me steadily and I slowly released the grip I had on his arm. I didn't doubt him. "Hide here until I return."

I swallowed hard and nodded. I could wait here . . . I would be fine . . . He'd come back to me.

I climbed the mossy embankment. Every step forward was a thump in my chest. Not much further.

I stopped in place, turning my head in the direction I left my female. Anger and obsession battled. Just as it had reared its head when I first attempted to leave.

Return.

Conflicting desires thrummed through my veins. Cresting over the hill, I slowed again.

I chuffed out a loud breath. The heavy scent of flesh burning singed my senses. A sneeze crawled free. Loud and echoing. Charred remains littered the ground.

I slowed, lifting my muzzle into the air. Inhaling, I took in the vast array of scents narrowed in the direction I headed. Something had happened, yet I kept stopping instead of charging toward the scents and sounds of destruction ahead. I flicked my ears back.

None would find my human where I left her. I was sure of it—but if they did? I sniffed again. That was the scent of others of my species—

I sank my claws in and out of the soil. I snarled and lunged in the direction I left Mia.

What lay ahead did not matter. I would not risk my mate.

I HUDDLED WITH MY LEGS BENT TO MY CHEST AND arms wrapped around my knees. I should have worn something more substantial than a sweater and sweats. Maybe about like five pairs of layered sweaters would have been enough if I didn't have Fenrir keeping me warm.

I scrubbed my palms against my thighs to build friction. Fenrir had been gone for only a little while and I was itchy about it.

What if he left me?

Should I go search for him?

What if he was harmed and he *couldn't* return?

The thoughts wouldn't stop.

A grunt echoed to me. I held my breath, listening intently.

It echoed again.

"Fenrir?" I whispered. I received nothing in response. I crawled toward the ledge of the drop and poked my head out of the hiding spot. It had sounded pained and guttural. Had something happened to him? The thought pounded in my chest, raising my pulse. The scratch of claws glided against cement, the sound loud and screeching.

What if he was injured to the point that he was dragging himself? He would return for me, I knew he would, even if it meant he dragged his half-dead carcass back to me.

I couldn't live with myself if I didn't check if it was him. Just a quick peek. I nibbled on my lower lip. Images of his torn-up body lying in my shack kept floating to the forefront.

But if it wasn't him, I'd put myself in harm's way. Then Fenrir might end up killing me for putting myself in that position.

I tapped my finger on the cement edge as I weighed my next decision. Dropping my head forward, I let out a sharp breath. I wouldn't be able to climb up to this little hiding spot. And calling out for him just seemed stupid of me. No, I best wait for him. It'd only been a short while.

A sudden rumbling huff blew my hair back. He was back!

"Fe—" I screamed and pitched to the side. Claws slashed so close to my face I could almost feel them. I scrambled across the little cement patch so fast my pants ripped. The monster, one just like Fenrir bared teeth at me, lunging again. I tipped over the side of the ledge, my scrabbling hands scraping against the brick on the way to the ground. I landed on my feet so hard my ankle buckled and I staggered forward. But I couldn't focus on the agony.

There. I could hide in the small, jagged hole at the base of the broken cement. If it was deep enough, then the monster wouldn't be able to reach me. It was my only choice, out running it wasn't a possibility.

Sunlight beamed across the path, no longer hindered by the

tall buildings. The sun hung high in the sky, at the highest peak. Only a few feet left. I pushed my legs harder.

Breathing fluttered my hair to my cheeks.

Behind me.

I gritted my teeth. A few more steps. Claws sliced into my back. I screamed and the force of the blow spun me around and knocked me to the ground, causing me to land on my injured back.

A large beast stood bipedally. Looming over me.

It snarled, showing every bit of its sharp blood-coated teeth at me, eyes flaring with inhuman red light. Large, curved claws headed toward my face. Screaming, I threw myself backwards to avoid the hit.

I hurriedly scooted, using my heels to shove myself. Those claws would have taken my head off. I whimpered as the monster kept coming. The lycan, as I now knew they were called, was much smaller than Fenrir, but no less frightening. The monster's red glow flared. The brown-furred monster dropped to all fours.

"Don't—" Fangs sank into my ankle and I screamed. Vomit crawled up my throat. I'd never experienced such pain. I could no longer see because of the blinding tears. Shards of agony ripped up my leg. The teeth met resistance from my bones.

I could no longer breathe and my arms grew weak. I fell flat on my back with a thump. Instead of biting down harder, it removed its teeth with a wet suctioning sound. Blood leaked from my injury, painting the brown muzzle.

"You smell of male lycan." Male . . . that must mean she was a female. Her head twitched slightly to the left. She prowled closer so her face neared mine, hovering over my cheek. Her copper-tinged breath wafted across my face.

"You are not the human I have been hunting." The thick voice vibrated through my chest. Her clawed hand settled on my stomach. The sharp tips sank into my stomach. I cried out, scrunching my face with pain. Her weight turned excruciating while her eyes remained on me. A pop blazed agony through my side and I whimpered, unable to make more noise because my lungs emptied. Something else started to give under her weight.

I screamed, tears flooding my eyes.

The female lifted her head with a huff. I followed her gaze to a massive, black furred lycan.

Fenrir! I wanted to cry out for him, but I was paralyzed from agony. A human male lay in an unconscious pile at his feet.

Wait, he hadn't made any move toward me. He seemed calm —too calm. I returned my attention to the female standing over me. One of his species.

Would he turn from me to keep her? I curled my hands into fists.

A soft hum echoed from her chest.

"You," she said with a slight purr in her voice. With interest. The panic swelling in my chest combined with the shards of pain pinching my side, back and ankle.

TWENTY-THREE
FENRIR

Though I had been gone only a short time, my instincts had been right to guide me back. My mate lay under the female lycan, her large paw on her stomach, the tips of her talons piercing into her skin. Every miniscule part of me urged me forward. But she was much too close to that female's claws and already smelled too much of blood. I must tread with care. She could not be harmed further.

"Is this the human you hunted?" I nudged the limp male I had found cowering in the tree. The male I recognized. One of the scientists that reveled in cutting my torso open and searching through my organs.

A self-proclaimed scientist. He liked to talk while he performed procedures on me.

The lycan lifted her muzzle, breathing in deep.

"I know you," the female said, her fangs flashing. "They cut you open. Often. You never begged for freedom."

Her red eyes blazed bright and she moved.

My little human whimpered under the massive female's

weight settling on her leg and claws sinking into her skin. I swallowed a snarl.

"I do not beg." I rumbled with a low growl. Her tail swished and she lowered to all fours, avoiding Mia's head by a claw-length.

She released pheromones . . . they plumed from her in a thick wave. She wanted to mate with me. I sneered. The thick coat of her scent burned my nostrils. Having the opposite affect that they should.

I would revel in ripping this lycan apart for touching my human.

"He was one who harmed you. He entered where they held you." She must have also been trapped. "Yet, you will gift him to me?"

I sank my claws into the male and tossed him forward, away from Mia in an effort to get the lycan away from her.

"I will gift him to you." My patience frayed.

"I escaped. And I destroyed them all." Her muzzle lifted proudly and she shifted in place, causing more pain-filled sounds from Mia.

"You destroyed the humans?" I would keep her attention. Her claws were deep in my human's leg. I inhaled her blood and a snarl built in my throat. I managed to stifle it and kept still. Only my past practice with patience allowed me to not move. If I engaged her in a fight, Mia would fall to her claws.

The female lycan would remove her limb, and she would bleed—she would die.

"Come to my den. I will claim you as my mate," the female said.

I rose to both of my hind limbs. Looming over the female. Her muzzle wiggled as she sniffed in.

Finally, she removed her claws from my human's leg and took a step toward me. I had not looked at Mia because I would lose all control.

I only wanted my human safe.

"Fenrir?" My mate breathed. Her eyes had begun to leak. Rage fired through my limbs, and I lunged. Slicing my claws into the female lycan's chest, dragging her down and away from Mia.

Nothing would harm my female and live. I landed on her, my claws slicing deep into her chest. She screeched, slicing claws into my side, and ripping through my fur but I ignored it.

I dragged my claws upwards, opening her chest until it split wide. Her innards spilled out.

I sliced into her throat with the same momentum. Deeper and deeper until she lay still and lifeless under me. I would have liked to offer her a slow death, but my human awaited me. I tossed her head away from the rest of her body and shredded into the organ in the middle of her chest pumping blood through her. Just to be sure she was no more. I shook out my fur and blood went flying.

I approached my human, limp and laying on the floor. That foreign pressure in my insides throbbed fire through me. Only she had woken up this ache inside me. I carefully nudged her.

Her chest moved up and down with rhythm. I had studied the motion accompanied by soft inhalations while she slumbered before. A relaxing sound that soothed my urge to pace. She would live. The female lycan sliced into her body and it looked like there may be broken bones, but she would live. When I fed her my release, the bleeding cuts would also heal. But I must get her to safety and get her cleaned up.

A gasp came from behind me and I stiffened. Slowly I

turned. The male scientist gasped again, holding his chest. His eyes widened on me, and he began to desperately scoot backward. Approaching the male, I flicked my ears back and forth.

"I know you. Creature 523. They called you Fenrir—" He continued to drag himself, but he would not outrun me and he seemed to recognize this. "W-wait, wait, I can help you!"

A growl vibrated from my throat.

"How?" What would he spew from his filthy human *mouth*? I reached him and bared my teeth.

The sour scent of urine reeked from him. Monsters did not piss, we did not need to, everything we devoured was turned into an energy source. This human must not have fed on monster release recently if he could release urine this way. His chest puffed out and his heart thumped loud enough for me to hear.

"I can help you—"

I sliced my claws straight through his face, rupturing his skull.

"Not interested," I said. Just as with the female, I would have taken pleasure in doing the many things to him that he'd done to me. Ripping a rib out. Slicing his tongue . . . but my human was more important.

Returning to her side, I found her still unconscious. I carefully collected her against my chest, allowing her blood to seep into my fur. As I passed him, I forcefully stepped on the human's chest, reveling in the pop of his ribcage flattening under my weight.

I huddled my mate close to my chest.

Time to return her to our den.

She seemed fixated on cleaning herself off, which was why I now found myself poking at that lever she used to spit water. My claw gouged the metal, and I immediately retreated my paw. The round spout sputtered, and droplets came from its edges. Something was working if it was causing the water to come. Using the soft underside of my paw, I gently nudge the spout. This time, it sprayed without effort.

Water pelted the fur on my arm.

Success.

My tail swished behind me and a loud clatter exploded in the small space. I took care and still broke things, but I would move the hindering objects once my human was clean and healed. I reached her where I had set her at the edge of her nest.

With one claw, I tore away the barrier covering her thin flesh then collected my now bared human and returned to the water. Cradling her to my chest, I squeezed into the tight space under the water.

She groaned and nuzzled her small face to my chest. I released a pleasured vibration from my chest, running my paw down her back in a soothing motion. When she bathed me, she rubbed the little floral scented thing all over me. I plucked it up with two of my claws and rubbed the end of it down her spine. She bathed me with such care, yet, I could not do the same to her because of my claws.

I clicked my teeth together and struggled to rub the thing on her head. My claws sliced through the soap, and it thudded on the ground. I snarled. I did the best I could and at least she no longer had blood crusting her body.

I forced my attention away from the cuts. I did not like seeing them on her, but now that she was no longer crusted from blood, her wounds were exposed. Wounds that needed to be healed.

A twitch of my claw on the lever in the opposite direction shut off the water. I shook my head, sending water spraying and my antlers gouged into the side of the box. She was very protective of her den. I must take more care.

Stepping out, I pulled a cloth over her as she had done before and the fibers collected the water.

With a few strides I returned to her nest and carefully set her down and the cloth fell aside, leaving her bare to me. Her breasts continued to call my attention. The tip, her nipples, were peaked. The reactive little flesh . . . I leaned over her to lick one. She groaned and as if calling it forth, my member emerged from my slit. I licked her again and her nipples puckered more.

My hips twitched forward as if I were mounting her. I would claim her, but she must be healed first. Slick coated my tip, and I guided it to her lips. I used the back of my claw to move her slumbering face to the side. Upon prodding her lips with the wet tip, her mouth opened. A guttural sound left me.

Half growl, half snarl. In her sleep, she lapped the tip, her mouth suckling.

I gripped my cock in hand and stroked down to my knot. It twitched in my hand, releasing more of my release into her mouth. She continued to suckle me, swallowing as I offered her more nectar.

I watched as her injuries knit closed until she no longer bled. A satisfied chuff left my muzzle, and I squeezed my knot. Her breasts moved with each of her inhales. I swelled and my release ripped through my member and buckled my knees. I grunted, leaning over her to sink my paw onto her nest. I heaved out breaths as my need gushed from me with painful ecstasy. I pulled my cock from her mouth and my release splashed across her chest, painting her in ribbons of my claim.

Setting my other paw down, my torso curved over where she rested at the edge of the nest, while my hind paws remained on the ground. I panted as the wave of ecstasy receded.

Her small hand slid across her belly, rubbing my need into her flesh. A vibration left my chest. I liked that. As if reacting to my sound, she sighed.

I breathed in her slick. She required release even while slumbering. Strange little human, but I would do whatever she needed. Straightening over her, I studied her small face with my liquid trickling from the corner of her mouth. She was covered in my release.

Dropping to all fours, I moved to the side where her legs hung and her strange, bare, and clawless back paws. I nestled my muzzle between her legs, and they fell apart. The sweet smell of her slick sent shockwaves through my cock. I glided my tongue up the leaking slit, collecting all of her need. I delved my tongue inside her, where my sex fit within. She gasped and her inner walls clamped onto my tongue.

I continued the steady licks, watching her features twist and panting breaths leave her lips. Her breasts moved up and down mesmerizingly. Mia cried out, her sound guttural and needy, making my cock release droplets from the tip. The flesh around my tongue squeezed with rhythmic pulses. Her head thrashed side to side as she reached her pleasure.

I retreated, satisfied, while my human remained slumbering. Her wounds no longer spilled blood. She should be completely healed.

Lifting to my hind paws, I stretched to lean over her face. I wanted in her, to feel her all around me after she was almost taken from me. The fur on the back of my neck stood and I slid my cock into her channel until she enveloped my knot. She took me where I belonged.

She sighed and her fingers sank into the fur of my belly, holding me to her. I cradled her to my chest and lay back so she rested on top of me.

With her sex hugging my cock, I curled my arms around her back, protecting her.

This here, her release—her pleasure, *her*, I hungered for all of it. Complete vengeance hadn't been dealt by my claws. That scientist had only been a segment of my retribution, but it did not matter any longer.

Mia sighed, her fingers digging into the fur on my chest to scratch my flesh with her miniature claws. She claimed me as wholly as I claimed her.

She writhed on my cock and her tight sheath clutched me— owning me—making a point. My knot throbbed inside her and my hips bucked.

She would need another rinse under the water once I finished with her.

TWENTY-FIVE
MIA

Tendrils of awareness crept over me in fragments. I wiggled my toes. Every inch of my body hurt. The female lycan.

My eyes popped open and I yanked the blanket off to look at my side. I expected to see blood and injuries that female gave me, but there were no open wounds. And other than my body aching, I felt pretty whole. And I was naked. I sniffed my arm.

I smelled like my home-made mint and lavender soap. I lifted my fingertips to my hair. The strands were damp.

I'd been bathed.

And I was still alive.

I'd passed out sometime after she offered to take Fenrir as her mate. He hadn't attacked her. He almost seemed . . . interested. I stiffened. Had they brought me back for a late snack?

I sat up in the creaky bed. Fenrir suddenly appeared a few feet away, his large body looming. I screamed and yanked my legs to my chest. He'd been laying on the ground beside my bed.

Dying naked seemed especially cruel. I scrunched my eyes shut. Fur touched my leg.

A whimper slipped free.

"What are you doing?"

His question came with such aggression. He'd already changed on me. He no longer needed me. Tears flooded my eyes. A wet nose bopped my forehead. My eyes popped open. Fenrir watched me steadily, his ears flicking.

"Why are you leaking?" He huffed. "Crying, I mean."

"I'm scared," I croaked.

His head cocked.

I blinked, a little lost.

His tongue flicked out to collect some tears that fell from my chin. The loud silence forced me to peek through my eyelashes.

Fenrir watched me steadily.

"No harm will ever come to you."

I was so confused.

"Y-you didn't bring the female lycan with you?" My voice tilted higher toward the ending syllable.

His head jerked back.

"No. I gutted her." The tufts over his eyes twitched down, causing his eyelids to lower over his glowing eyes.

"You did?" I couldn't contain my shock. "I-I thought you would mate her—"

"You wanted me to mate with her?" He roared and his head drew back further, his large fangs showing a bit too much.

"I didn't *want* that. I thought you would prefer someone of your species—"

"Species," he snarled. "You want a male of your species?"

"What?" I gasped. "I don't *want* anything!"

The bed creaked under his weight, causing me to jostle side to side as the mattress shuddered. I flattened on my back as he leaned over me. His sharp fangs hovered much too close. The glow from his eyes flared and the tip of his antlers scraped across the headboard. I winced at the marks.

"You are mine. No other will touch you."

It seemed like a threat *and* a promise.

He said he would protect me, always. His body remained stiff and unyielding. He didn't soften, as if my questions and assumptions had angered him.

I pressed my palm to his chest gingerly.

He stiffened and snapped his teeth at me.

"I'm sorry," I said, rushed.

He continued looking at me as if I spoke a foreign language, and I supposed, to him, I was.

"You believed I would leave you?" He huffed and it sounded an awful lot like disgust. "I will kill anything that attempts to take you from me—"

I tugged at the fur on his chest to hoist myself up to cling to his neck. I exhaled noisily.

"Thank you. Thank you." I mumbled into his fur. "I don't want another. Just you." I closed my eyes tightly. He could have easily left me, a weaker being than him, to turn to the female of his kind, but he hadn't. He cared for me as much as I cared for him.

The stiffness incrementally faded from his limbs and his weight settled on top of me.

I didn't want to leave him, and I didn't care if that made me messed up in the head. I'd never experienced such safety and peace in another's presence.

"I must taste you." I sucked in a breath, a flush traveling

down my body. Fenrir slowly inched down my body until he hovered over my sex. Licking my lips, I spread my knees.

I couldn't stop breathing hard. He hovered over my mound, his eyes still on me. He breathed out so hard that the warm breath tickled my skin and rustled my pubic hair. My face warmed.

His desire for me was a tangible thing that sent shockwaves of pleasure through my system. I wanted him more than I knew how to express.

With his antlers within reach, I grabbed hold and forced his mouth between my legs. His wet tongue licked my damp core and I arched my back, shuddering with a loud moan. The smooth glide of his tongue delved into every crevice. It felt raw and sensitive, but his careful laps soothed the ache away.

"More, Fenrir," I begged.

He growled, loud, intimidating, feral, and his tongue flicked against my achy sex with quick lashing swipes. The flat of his tongue flicked against the nerves that set me aflame. I cried out, thrashing my head side to side.

His hips jerked forward and the bed jostled. He groaned, thrusting against my bed, moving the entire frame, causing my breasts to bounce.

"Fenrir," I moaned.

His tail flicked behind him. The sight of his excitement enflamed mine. His canine fangs rubbed against my flesh. Such dangerous big teeth . . . The orgasm slammed into me. My torso arched. His warm grip forced my hips down and he turned his head to flick his tongue inside my throbbing channel. My sex clasped onto his tongue repeatedly, attempting to keep him inside me.

The electricity eventually subsided, but what didn't was the speed of his licks. My thighs shook with the over sensitivity. I tugged on his antlers until he stopped to look up at me.

"I want to taste you." I breathed. His head cocked. I patted the bed. "Lay down." He slowly did as I ordered as we switched spots. He lay on his back, slightly lower to accommodate his antlers. The bend of the back of his knee rested on the edge of the bed. I perched at the end of the bed. Staring at his bobbing, slick cock. I licked my lips. He was scary big.

I wrapped both hands around his base, right above his forming knot. I struggled to hold the girth. Glowing cum trickled from the tip, and his slick member throbbed under my touch. I cleaned the liquid, humming at the sweet taste. Fenrir's teeth flashed and his hips jerked up toward my mouth, but I retreated and worked to hide my smile. I loved driving him mad with lust.

His palm pressed down on the back of my head, the tips of his claws rubbing against my scalp and neck. He insistently nudged my head down, dragging me to his thick, throbbing cock. More glowing cum leaked from the tip, the liquid shining on his mushroom tip. I fit my mouth around his seam and flicked my tongue along the silky texture.

He groaned and arched his hips. I rubbed my palms down his length. Whines spilled from his muzzle. His arms dropped to his sides and his claws speared into the mattress. He sounded so needy and crazed. His sounds caused a wave of moisture to wet my inner thighs. My channel throbbed, wanting him deep inside. But this was about him. Driving *him* crazy. I enjoyed watching his loss of control. Him becoming a whimpering, needy mess under me.

He was submitting to me. And it made me feel so powerful. This monster was a gift.

"Lick my knot."

I pulled up with a pop of my lips and began to lick my way down his slippery slickness. I dipped my tongue into the crevice of his knot before it ballooned outward. He grunted, hips jerking.

He was close to release.

Fenrir stiffened and I dragged my mouth up the shaft. I wrapped my lips around him, flicking the flat of my tongue against his tip.

He roared and I swore our house vibrated from the force. Liquid jutted from him in a rush, spilling into my mouth, but it was too much. I couldn't swallow it all in time for it not to spill so it painted my chin and breasts.

His glowing eyes flared brightly as did the bright fur interwoven with his dark pelt. His chest rose and fell with rapid pumps. He lay panting—spent.

I grinned up at him, satisfied.

"Fenrir, keep it steady," I chastised. He grunted. I swore he was exasperated with me, but every time I peeked at him, there was no indication of it.

His huffs wouldn't fool me. The grumpy lycan seemed to only have that setting, but I knew him. It was all bluster. He would do anything for me, quite literally. In the time we'd been together, he'd shown me that.

He made everything so much easier. Carrying water up to the house from the well was no longer a daunting process. All I had to do was ask Fenrir. He was learning slowly but surely. And as he learned, we built our home together.

We were happy choosing each other over anyone, even those of our own species. I grinned at his back as he lowered the basket he carried that was full to the brim with freshly plucked corn for the animal feed. He'd already dropped two of them behind us.

I couldn't take my eyes off his broad body. Such a big . . .

He slowed and turned toward me. He sniffed, and his head

cocked. Fenrir set the basket on the ground and slowly approached on all fours, his tail flicking behind him.

I ran my fingers up his muzzle. He leaned into my touch as I trailed my fingers up into the fur right under his pointed ears.

An engine-like purr vibrated his body. Oh no, he only did that when he was especially pleased. My body recognize his desire. I squeezed my legs tightly together. Maybe he wouldn't smell my lust since the wind was blowing hard.

"You should, uh, grab the basket . . ." His nose nudged my belly. I took hold of the smooth base of his antlers and leaned back before they poked my eye out. "Fenrir," I said again. Not knowing what exactly I was asking for.

"My human needs me." Fenrir's arm wrapped around me, and he brought me to the ground with ease and care. He reared over me, his glow bright and blinding, forcing my gaze to his sharp teeth. The big, bad lycan was in a mischievous mood. I grinned up at him.

And he was all mine.

THANK YOU FOR READING!

Visit my website for more book information and be sure to join my reader group and follow my social media platforms to keep up with my releases.

ACKNOWLEDGMENTS

To my Lycan teams—You are all amazing! Thank you so much for taking the time to read my books and sharing your thoughts with me. I appreciate every single one of you.

Aaron, thank you for supporting my dreams and picking up my slack when I'm busy in the writing cave.

Como siempre, gracias a mi mamá y mi papá.

Allie obsessively reads books featuring sexy, possessive heroes and headstrong heroines. So, it's no wonder characters just like that bustle to escape her imagination.

When she's not working away at her keyboard, she can be found in bed with a good book or bingeing shows.